ALL DARK

STILL SURVIVING BOOK 2

BOYD CRAVEN III

 Created with Vellum

PROLOGUE

I REMEMBER the song "A country boy can survive." I'm not sure how good I'm doing according to the lyrics. I've survived all right, but do I still have my humanity?

When the solar storm knocked out the power, seemingly nationwide, the fall of normalcy seemed to happen quickly for everyone else. For me, at my grandparents' old homestead, it was a minor inconvenience. I've been a lot of things in my life—a poacher, a moonshiner and, although I break the law, I always try to follow what's morally and ethically correct. Not all laws are, so I only tend to break the ones I need to for my family's survival, and only so long as it doesn't harm anyone else.

In the course of helping friends and family, I'd shot and killed a man who'd been pursuing Lester, Grandpa's oldest friend, and cutout for our 'shining business.

Turned out, his favorite nephew was the head of law enforcement for the area. Imagine my shock when he'd showed up to the homestead one day with Jessica, Lester, and everyone else. Now? All law enforcement seems to have been pulled into the larger towns, cities, and camps as the federal government tries to get a handle on the worsening situation. My family can live without power for a long time if we're careful, but not everyone else can.

Let's back things up though and reflect on how much has changed. I'd been working toward a degree in chemical engineering, ending up with a teaching job to start this coming fall, and run across an old high school crush. To top things off, I'd finally bullied my grandpa into going to the doctor's office where we've hopefully found his cancer in time. I did what I had to do to get his surgery and treatment paid off by setting up the biggest run of hooch Grandpa and I had ever considered. Then, one day in the barn, I was adopted by a juvenile German Shepherd, Raider. He's been my companion, protector, and faithful friend throughout all of this.

The biggest thing that worries me is Lance's Hillbilly Mafia and their treatment of locals. It didn't take him long to embrace lawlessness when the lights went out for good. Before that, he'd been nothing more than a honky tonk owner and former boyfriend of Jess. That alone was enough to put a black mark against him, but growing up, I hated him as well. He'd kidnapped friends of Jess and I, torturing them for information about their food storage. That was why I hadn't hesitated when the man on the four-wheeler had been chasing and shooting at Les's SUV. If I had done nothing, he would have probably been cornered and killed. I shouldn't feel guilty that three the father of one of the three little girls had died while I was protecting one of mine, should I? One man or three?

1

I RODE my bike back to our homestead with a heavy heart. If I were trying to be cool, I'd say I was doing that so the noise of the wind blowing across my face would prevent me from hearing anything, but if I was telling the truth... I'd let the man I'd killed go out of my thoughts. He'd been chasing Lester, shooting at a family friend, and I'd done what I had to do to save a friend. I was sure my shot had been the one to kill the man on the quad and wondered which of the little girls he had fathered.

Once the little girls back at the farm had devoured all the quick food I had given them. I'd pulled out the Ziploc baggies of rice and oatmeal I always carried in my backpack. The rice was minute rice and the oatmeal was instant, but all of it could be made with minimal cooking and smell. I'd given them to the girls who took off for the house, yelling for their mothers. From what little they'd said, I knew there were at least two younger boys on the farm, their grandpa, and mothers. No more fathers though, Jess' group and I had killed them in a running gunfight while they chased Lester Doyle onto our property.

We'd buried their fathers almost in the front yard, up the slope near the road. Had they been trying to ambush and kill Lester for what he had? Was it a case of mistaken identity? In reality, Lester was an old criminal the same way my grandpa and I were. It was possible he'd been recognized and, just like in the fiction books I'd read, someone may have been looking to settle some scores.

But now... The kids were starving. It wasn't their fault. What I'd given them today was enough for a day or two for me. It was part of my seventy-two-hour kit, but the kids had treated the bags of food like they were gold. I needed to scoot out of there. Raider kept pace with me easily. Hell, a turtle going fast could have kept pace with me. Even though I was stuck deep in my head, thinking heavy thoughts, I wasn't so far gone that I didn't hear the sound of motors coming up behind me.

"Raider, come," I said sharply, and went off the road.

The tall grass on the shoulder had dried in the summer heat, and I hoped I wasn't making too much of a path; that'd be easily noticed. The motors sounded gas powered and rough running. I pushed my bike behind a clump of tall grass that had taken root around some saplings. I laid it down flat and was about to call to Raider, but saw he was already staring at me, his head cocked to the side. I didn't have much time.

"Come here, boy, down. We're going to hide, just like we did before."

I was already pulling my pack off and had my rifle laid out in front of me. The old 25-.270 looked ugly in the dried grass. It wasn't as lush here as it had been near the Mueller farm. I pulled my camo netting off and shook it out. I had about ten seconds until the vehicle or vehicles crested to rise. Lucky for me, I was on the bottom slope of the hill so anybody coming from either way wouldn't see me.

Seven seconds. The net was out, and I was shaking it to get enough coverage to go over me and the bike. I'd lay on the damned thing if I had to.

Five seconds. It didn't come undone all the way. Dammit.

Two seconds. I laid across my bike, pulling the net over my body and head, leaving the end of the barrel poking out.

I saw a sparkle of chrome as Raider crawled underneath the netting with me and gave me a chuff as if to say, ain't I a good boy? I was holding my breath and knew any large movement at this point would do more to draw the eye of whomever was coming down the old dirt road. In my right peripheral vision I saw two motorcycles bearing down on me. These weren't cute dirt bikes; they were Harley Davidsons. I'd looked at these exact models myself once, the 1200 Sportsters, a no frills bike that I had planned on buying when I could afford it.

Both bikes were black and ridden by two regular looking guys. They didn't have fancy leathers or vests on, just denim and plaid shirts. Both men, at a quick glance, looked Caucasian or Hispanic. One of them wore a blue bandana and a pair of sunglasses. I got a real good look at them when they stopped about ten feet away from me. I trembled and got the rifle ready. Raider was tense but quiet, even his breathing had slowed.

The man in the bandana pulled a radio off his right side and turned off his bike. After a moment, his partner did as well.

"Blue team has done a drive-by," he said into the handheld.

"What's the place look like?" The volume was turned way up on the handheld and the man was holding it to his ear, probably deafened from the bike's chopped pipes.

"Old farm looks like they have soybean or some kind of corn poking up. Nothing ready to harvest."

The reply was a string of curses. Raider started to

growl, but I shushed him as quietly as I could. Only ten feet away, and neither man flinched. Those bikes were very loud. I had the rifle more or less pointed in their direction, and I'd had my can on the end already. I didn't like the sound of 'blue team' and what sounded like a recon report.

"Had kids start to run down the driveway, but two ladies came running out after them screaming bloody murder. When they saw the bikes, all of them took off into the tree line."

"Were the men there?" The radio crackled.

"I didn't see them. We didn't stop and take a longer look because they might have been waiting in ambush. Wanted to look as casual as possible."

The radio crackled, and this time it was a lot clearer, as somebody transmitting closer to them got on. "How old were the women?" a rough voice asked.

"Twenty or thirty, or maybe forty. Old enough, but not used up," the second man said, hitting bandana on the shoulder with a grin.

"The right age," Bandana said, without looking at his partner. "We went a couple miles past the farm. Doesn't look like there's anybody else in the area, but we didn't want to stop and kick in random doors to find out."

"Right age? You mean breathing?" His partner laughed at his own joke.

"Last time I tell you, Danny, you sicko, you ever even look at one of the young—"

"Do a drive-by again, slower. See if anybody responds," the first voice on the radio told them.

"Got it, boss," Bandana said, and started turning the knob when it crackled again.

He hurried and turned the volume back up. "What's that, boss? I missed that last message."

"You see that Marshall bastard yet?"

"No," he said into the handset, "but if I do, how do you want me to uh... take care of that particular problem?"

"He can't be dead. The little fucker should have been choked out on day one, but it's Lance's favorite cousin. If he realizes that we don't have the kid anymore..."

"Got it, boss. And about the farm? They have to know we're going to be back..."

"Yeah, ask him about the farm and the women and the kids—"

"Go ahead and get rolling, blue team. Change your gear out when you get back and rest. You'll be heading back that way in two days."

"Got it, boss. Blue team out," he said, turning the knob off and then putting it back on his belt. "Danny, you sick fuck, you keep talking shit like that and I'll bury you like I did your idiot cousin."

Bandana was mad, and his hands were shaking.

"Yo Momma," the other shot back in a pique of immaturity that would almost have had me laughing if the situation hadn't been so dire.

They were going to hit the farm. It was defenseless and everyone there was probably weak and malnourished, if the kids were any indication. At least one of them sounded like a predator, and Marshall? Wasn't that the kid who'd broken into the barn?

As they fired up the hogs, I pieced together the puzzle. Whoever 'Boss' was, he'd taken Marshall, Lance's cousin. To top that off, they were planning what sounded like a raid on the farm, for supplies, and if what the sicko was saying, the women and children. I got a sick feeling in my stomach.

I know there was one old man there, but the wives and kids were alone other than that. I needed more information, and I needed to get in touch with Jess. I had left the radio back at the homestead with Grandpa and Grandma in case they needed to call in help. I needed to get home, and fast!

"Raider, good boy," I said, petting him before lifting the camo netting and getting off the bike.

Raider bounded to his feet and spun around in a happy circle as I got to my feet stiffly. I'd been laying across one of the pedals, and it had dug into my side. Raider watched me put my pack and rifle back on before picking up my bike and righting it. I could hear the motorcycles still, but they were headed the other way, slowly.

"We have to get back home. You think you can keep up?" I asked him, pushing my bike into the road.

Raider made a disgusted snort, rubbed a paw over his nose, then sat and waited for me to mount up.

"I take it you think you can beat me?" I asked him.

He shot ahead, a furry streak. I hurriedly followed.

2

Raider surprised me, and I didn't let up on the pedal pounding. If anything, he set the pace and it was one that had my heart racing and my blood pumping as I was finally forced to slow to make the turn into the driveway. The furry missile ran full tilt to the front porch and sat, waiting for me. I got there several seconds later, my chest heaving. I got off the bike and leaned it against the railing then took off the rifle. The door opened, and Grandpa made a gimme motion, so I handed it to him before pulling off my pack.

"You weren't gone long," Grandpa told me, rubbing his stomach.

"Got news," I told him, panting.

"Best come in. Grandma made you a thermos, but you didn't take it."

"No ice. Besides, I wasn't sure how long I was going to be gone and—"

"Wes," Grandma said, pushing Grandpa out of the way, and wrapped me in a hug.

I hugged her back, dropping my pack on the porch. "Hi, Grandma."

"Come inside, take some layers off. I can smell the sweat."

She was right. I was dressed much too warmly for the weather, but I had been going for concealment and quiet, which meant my poaching gear.

I peeled the outer layers off and was left in a pair of basketball shorts and socks. I went to the pitcher and poured some out on my hand, then wiped down my face, the back of my neck, and splashed some under my arms. Grandma just shook her head and rolled her eyes. Grandpa was pulling down three glasses and the thermos of 'lemonade'.

"It's gotta be bad if you're so quiet," Grandpa started.

"Yes, come sit and catch a breeze in front of the window and tell us what you found out."

"The... The three men we killed were the old farmer's sons or sons-in-law. There are three ladies and at least five to seven kids who are wondering what happened to them."

"They were shooting at Les, chased him all the way here," Grandma said.

"Yeah, but I think Lance and the guys who are with him may have gone there to try to take stuff before—"

"How do you know that?" Grandpa interrupted, an eyebrow raised.

"Two guys on Harleys, had to ditch my bike in the tall grass and hide. They stopped right beside of me and got on the radio," I told him the rest as he poured me a large cup of the nectar.

I told him how it sounded like they had done a probing action there before and how they were likely to be doing it again, if not an outright attack, in two days. I worried that they thought Lester's SUV was one of Lance's and they were retaliating, not raiding. I wasn't sure about any of this, but there was one thing I was for sure of.

"If we hadn't killed their fathers, would those kids still be hungry?" I asked them both.

Grandma had been fanning her face with an old *Time* magazine, but she stopped at my question. Grandpa opened his mouth to answer, then shut it and took a long drink of the warm lemonade that had been fortified with whiskey.

"They were trying to kill Lester," Grandpa said again. "No use in feeling guilty for saving a friend's life."

"Is it that easy though? What about the kids? Grandpa, you should see those little girls. They look like they're two meals away from starvation."

15

Grandpa looked to the side, then to Grandma. Raider decided he was done waiting on us and walked to me, flopped on his back and put all four paws up, kicking with all feet until I reached down and gave his stomach a rub. He let out a yawning sound that sounded strangely human. I took a sip and waited.

"And you say they are going to be attacked in two days?"

"The guys were ten feet away from me tops. I could hear the radio clearly."

Grandma reached over and took my glass and downed it, then refilled it and handed it back to me. I watched as she shuddered as the warmth spread through her. She joked and complained about Grandpa having a drink or two and hardly ever gave me any grief... yet she was the first one to make the specialty recipes, with her lemonade being my personal favorite.

"What do you want to do about it?" Grandma asked.

"I want to get ahold of Jess and see if their group can help, warn the families what's coming."

"I'll get the radio," Grandpa said simply.

"I was worried about something like this," Jess' voice came out of the handset.

"Same here," another voice chimed in; her father's?

"I'm heading back to the homestead to warn them," I said over the radio.

"That wouldn't be a good idea—" Jess was interrupted.

"No, let us make contact," the male voice said.

"I... ok." I took a long swallow.

I'd switched from the lemonade to some water I'd just drawn from the hand pump, the coldest thing available without refrigeration, and was sitting out on the front porch, my big rifle leaned against the railing.

"We'll make contact and advise them to move on. With the numbers Lance's group has, and how it's growing, that's all we can do," Jess said.

"I want to run them out some food," I said.

There was silence. Raider was laying in the shade made by the corner of the overhanging roof of the porch, sleeping. I wished I was; my emotions were a mess, and I was having a hard time sorting out the growing sense of panic in my gut.

"That wouldn't be a good idea," Jess said finally.

"Why not?" I asked her, anger creeping into my voice.

"Too much to get into over the radio," her father's voice cut in, "so let us handle it."

"They're... you know what... there are two days left. Unless you guys are rolling out, right now, get in touch with me the same time tomorrow night."

"Wes, don't do anything stu—"

It hurt to cut off Jess' words when I turned off the radio. I wanted to throw it, but realized it would be a dramatic gesture that would do nobody any good. I also realized that I wasn't even mad at them necessarily. I could think of a dozen reasons on why going back with food was a bad idea, but I felt responsible. I'd killed one of their fathers. I was sure of it. There were a few things in life that I was naturally good at: making moonshine, my studies in chemistry, and shooting. Two of the three were essential life skills, and the latter the reason I was sure I'd had the kill shot.

Had they been chasing Les off because they'd been attacked once already, and thought he was with them? Did they think the old man driving slowly down the road meant he'd been casing their place out? Or simply, were they hoping to gun him down, and take his SUV and any and all supplies they could get from him? My head swam, and I drained the water glass. I needed more if I was going to do what I wanted, and I didn't have a lot of time.

"You're going back anyway?" Grandpa asked me.

"Yes," I said, waiting for the ass chewing I knew I was coming.

"Even though it may not do one lick of a bit of difference and put your own safety in jeopardy?"

"Grandpa, I have to," I told him simply, meeting his gaze.

He'd been standing in the doorway, leaning against it. Already, I could see the life coming back into him after the surgery. The hollowed-out eyes weren't so hollow anymore, and his loose skin was starting to fill out around his neck and face as he gained back much needed weight.

"Boy, did it ever occur to you that if you get yourself hurt or killed out there, it might not be the best for me and your grandma?"

"I promise I'll be careful," I told him.

He nodded again. "Good. Your grandma and I been sitting in there chewing on this while you had your radio call. I think we should move the coop and get a few of your buckets out for ourselves. We also think it might not be a horrible idea if you mosey on up there and make sure they are all right."

That about rocked me off my feet. I was expecting more logic and reasoning. I was acting on feeling and instinct.

"I want to load part of my pack up with dry goods when I go," I told him.

"You do that, and if they got little 'uns... If they ain't got no place to go..."

"Grandpa, that's asking a lot of you and Grandma—"

"Don't you sass your grandpa none," Grandma said, coming into the open doorway, putting her arms around Grandpa's still skinny chest.

"Yes, ma'am," I said, tipping my hat. "This trip... I think I'm going to have Raider stay here with you. I'm only going to bike part of the way in. If they are watching the farm..."

"You're worried about being spotted?" Grandma asked.

I nodded, and she disappeared, only to be back a moment later. My overalls were damp at the cuffs, but she'd rinsed them out in the sink. They were wool, and in a color that naturally blended in. I'd need my boots and hat to finish things off.

"You want my hunting suit?" Grandpa asked me suddenly.

"Your..." Then it hit me. He'd taken camo netting and made his own ghillie suit. I usually didn't like to use it, but with the sun beating down on me and as hot as mine was, if I could put up with the annoying, itchy, scratchy feeling of the wool, I could put up with Grandpa's suit. I just didn't like how it covered my face and made access to my pockets a pain. "I think I'll stick with what I know for now," I told him after thinking about it.

He nodded and headed into the house. He came back a moment later with his suppressed .25/270 and two boxes of his hand-loaded ammunition. I took the overalls and laid them out across the porch to finish drying and left my deer gun where it was. I had a coop to move.

THE TRACTOR FIRED up a lot easier than I ever would
have imagined. I worried about the sound traveling,
but we needed the forks on the front of the tractor to
move the coop off the doors to the root cellar. Raider
ran beside the tractor, then took off like a shot as a
rabbit was scared into bolting for new cover. I watched
for a moment as he ran it down. Two large bites and it
looked like he swallowed it whole. Moving the coop
itself didn't take long, and Foghorn kept a wary eye on
me. With a full belly, Raider wasn't really looking at
the rooster, but was nearby, as if to comfort me with his
presence again.

The tiny, evolved velociraptors all crowded the
coop to see what I was doing, even while the tractor
was running. I grimaced when I got it free and saw the
deep litter covering the doors. Grandma was going to

have a field day, and I knew who was going to have to scrub the mess clean when things calmed a bit. I headed down with Grandpa following me.

He saw what was down there and whistled. "I knew you had a ton of stuff, but I never realized it was this much."

"Buckets everywhere," I said absentmindedly. "There we go." I went to a stack that had several open at the top.

It was what I'd left open and unsealed for immediate use after the National Guard units were done searching the area. I had a pocketful of one-gallon Ziploc baggies which I started filling from the first open bucket. Two gallons worth of rice in two bags. Next was mixed beans, though most of them were northern dried beans from the last shipment I'd gotten from Margie and Curt's bakery. I filled a bag up with those. Then I went to one more bucket and filled a bag with lentils.

"You getting them some toilet paper after the shits you're about to give them?" Grandpa asked me.

I turned to give him a snarky remark, but saw he was grinning. "They can use a leaf, just like we're going to have to soon."

"What, you didn't prep with toilet paper?" Grandpa asked, looking through the supplies with an alarmed expression on his face.

"Nope," I lied, laughing inside.

He started cursing as I made my way to a sealed bucket, one of the last I'd packed. It was the mixed nuts. I hadn't thought I'd ever be able to use them all up before they went rancid, but I realized what a gold mine it actually was. Protein and fats, portable, shelf stable for a time. I filled two of the Ziploc baggies before sealing them. Grandpa grabbed a few bags and I gathered the rest, and we made our way out to see Raider and Foghorn nose to beak outside.

"They've been like that since you went down," Grandma said.

"I... Raider, leave him alone."

Raider made a weird mewling sound, but he never turned his head from the rooster that was nearly the same size as his head.

"They're just having a staring contest. I don't have the heart to tell your loco dog that Foghorn is blind in that eye though."

"What?" I asked, snorting.

"Why do you think he walks in a circle around you? He's keeping his good eye on you. Can't see out the left side."

I grinned and shook my head. I had no idea if he was pulling my leg or not, but the laughter felt like a releasing of tension after feeling as if my heart had been crushed. I turned to look back at the open Bilco doors, but Grandpa was already waving me to the porch. Grandma had taken my canteen, and I could see her working the hand pump. I was about to rush over to take over for her when I saw her quit.

"Aren't you going to tell me this is a bad idea?" I asked Grandpa as Grandma walked back, capping the old metal lid.

"Son, we all know it's a bad idea," he said, lining the bags up on the railing on the porch.

"I knew it was a horrid idea as soon as you started telling me the story," Grandma said, as if to finish Grandpa's thought.

"Then why are you—"

"Could you live with yourself if you did nothing?" Grandpa interrupted.

"I... no." I admitted.

"This is one of those times you're doing the wrong thing for the right reasons, and your heart's in the right place. Most of the time, you'll get your ass handed to you, but sometimes, things work out ok. I don't want to see you hurt none, but in life..."

Grandma picked up next, "Sometimes you just have to do it, or knowing you could have done something and didn't... it eats at you. Changes you in a way we don't want to see you have to change."

Grandpa nodded, Raider let out a chuffing sound, and I saw he'd abandoned the staring match with Foghorn and was standing beside Grandma. He'd snuck up, quiet as all get out, and I hadn't caught him moving in my peripheral vision. I grabbed my pack and opened it up with one hand, shoving the baggies of food in. Grandpa handed me the bags he'd laid down a moment before, and those went in as well. Last was one of the boxes of the wildcat hand-loads. The other I'd keep in an outer pouch after I'd made sure everything was loaded up.

"Thanks," I told both of them suddenly.

My entire life, they'd loved and raised me. It wasn't a perfect life, but I couldn't imagine anything better, and the fact they understood and could empathize with how torn up I was about this decision was more than touching. In fact, there was some stupid wind blowing and some grit was getting into my eyes. I wiped at them, then pulled my camo netting to me and unrolled it with my back facing the wind.

"You going to tell them what happened to their daddies?" Grandma asked me suddenly.

"No," I told her softly, "that isn't my place. I'll tell their mothers if I run into them. Hell, I have to. You heard Jess and her dad on the radio. They... I don't know..." The anger was bubbling up inside of me. "I need to do this, and I don't think they're going to help."

"Sometimes a man has to walk his own path," Grandma said solemnly.

"Where'd you hear that?" Grandpa asked her.

"I don't know, I think it was in one of your Playboys you left out the other night? Nothing else to read while you're snoring up a storm. Farting in your sleep and—"

"That's way too much information," I cut her off.

"Wow," Grandpa said and put both hands up as if to ward off an attack. "Raider, come inside and get some water."

I watched as his ears perked up at that, then saw him looking at me questioningly. I nodded to him, and he went for the front door that Grandpa was pushing open for him. He slipped inside, and the door closed behind him on the springs.

"Want me to put the coop back in place?" I asked suddenly.

"Naw, don't want to fire up the tractor again right away, just in case somebody is looking for the sound of where it came from the first time. We'll get it another day."

That made sense to me and I nodded, before walking over and hugging him then Grandma. I had to get out of here before I choked up. I checked the rifle, then finished loading up. I could hear Raider barking his fool head off as I rode away. I hoped I would see him again. Even though I knew I was doing the right thing, I felt like I was going to pay for my decision, and painfully. Feeling like I had a target on my back, I started pedaling harder. I prayed I would have an uneventful trip.

I HAD SET UP IN THE SAME SPOT WHERE I HAD FIRST RUN across the kids. The farmhouse now looked like it had been shut up tight from the view I had with the scope. Shutters were drawn and the door that had looked to have been open in the distance was closed tightly. None of the kids were in sight. Things felt wrong. I held still and controlled my breathing, listening. I knew I was slightly upwind of the farm and would have preferred not to have been, but most people didn't consider their scent trail when stalking game, or in my case, sneaking up.

I'd tied the camo netting to my pack and had left it partially unrolled. The long grass that had been dead and dried out from the summer heat was stuck in parts of it here and there, almost like a ghillie suit. Grandpa's would have been great, but it was hot, and I didn't want to carry the extra weight. The fact that the farmhouse was now all shut up had me thinking that the family had holed up inside. Either I had spooked them, or Lance's boys on the motorcycles had.

I checked myself; they weren't Lance's boys if they had kidnapped Marshall. It sounded to me like they were holding him, to control Lance? To get his supplies? I wondered if that was what had made him act the way he had been, but only for a moment. I'd seen from his own actions that my version of 'break the law as long as it harms no one' didn't apply to him. He had no issue with that. I felt my side for Raider, then remembered he was back at the farm, watching over my grandparents. I'd liked to have stashed my backpack and done the creep to the house on my own, but I wanted and needed the supplies that were inside.

I slowly started making my way along the edge of the tall grass that separated their field from the wild bramble and raspberry bushes I was hiding in. To me, it looked like there was going to be a bumper crop of soybeans this fall, but without treatment, none of the food was edible. I remembered eating fresh soybeans as a kid, not knowing any better, and getting all kinds of stomach cramps and digestive issues. They needed to be processed properly, and simply soaking them was the start to a long process. Still, I saw no animals and no kitchen garden like we had.

"Raider buddy," I said to empty air. "If I'm about to do something stupid, speak up."

I knew I wasn't going to get an answer, so I crawled on my belly, the .25/270 in front of me. I moved slowly, ignoring the jumping insects and mosquitos that were trying to feast upon my arms and face. I had them covered, but they tried with a relentless pursuit of blood. Was that what I was waiting for when I made contact with the families? Could I trust the kids to carry the message to the grownups? I was approaching the farmhouse from the side, so I could see both the front door and the outline of a porch on the back that faced the old barns.

Their barn was much like ours, old boards, painted red, large rolling doors. The difference was that their barn was about three times the size of ours and the metal roofing had been done within the last decade or so. Ours was more functional, meant for a small farm's worth of livestock; whereas this one was to hold equipment. The rolling door was open, but I couldn't make anything out from my angle. My goal was the house, so I continued my slow crawl. Ten feet. Fifteen. Twenty. I had a thousand to go, and my approach would take me a long while if I continued at the slow, easy pace I was going.

"...Don't want to!" I heard a little girl's voice, then her scream of frustration.

She sounded familiar, was it the smaller girl I'd seen? Laney? Or was that Mary? I shook my head and tried to pinpoint where I'd heard that come from. It hadn't been the house, so I turned my focus to the barn. The barn was just as far as the house. If I followed the field, I could make better time by going through the edge, letting the tall grass mask my movements. I would be almost invisible from those angles as long as I stuck to the edge, using the tall grass as cover to conceal things. Impatience got the better of me, and I moved that way.

After a few moments, I got through and held still, scanning the field like I'd done dozens of times already. Immature plants were poking up and making their own cover. I could see in spots where something had dug up and wallowed in a low spot. Feral hogs? Hogs? I turned back to the house and barn. Seeing nothing, I started moving on all fours, keeping my rifle in front of me, the silencer pointed to my left.

"...Laney, don't you..."

A woman's voice called out as a young girl broke from the darkness of the barn. I watched as what looked like a young woman, judging by her figure, followed. The girl had something in her hand, held out in front of her, and was running like her life depended on it. The woman was slower, which made me slow to watch. I knew I was all but invisible, but I could see them good enough. The girl was shoving something in her mouth as the woman let out a grunt of frustration before stopping the chase and sitting down in the middle of the overgrown lawn in front of the barn. I was amazed at how much I could hear, but then again, there hadn't been any motorized sounds, no radios nor phones, for a long time now. My hearing had started picking up things again that it had once filtered out. I could hear the girl's feet pounding as she ran, and ran straight for me!

I went still as the woman called out to her again. She made her way to her feet, but I was watching the little one shove a handful to her mouth again before turning back to see if she was still being pursued. I was going to have to make a decision soon. Stay down, move out of the way, or show myself to the running girl. She made an almost direct beeline for my hiding spot. Again. They had done this earlier, and I had to wonder if what looked like a good place to move to the farm in concealment was also a favorite hiding spot of the kids. I cursed myself mentally and got lower to the ground and started moving again, hoping to get out of the way. The girl's fast feet had brought her closer to me, too close for my comfort.

"Laney!" a man's voice shouted, booming and echoing across the farm.

The little girl stopped as if poleaxed, her feet almost coming out from her. She turned, still putting something to her mouth. I could see her throat working as she swallowed something. I got the rifle up and made sure the safety was on and looked through the scope. I found her after a couple seconds; she was sweaty, her eyes and cheeks red as if she'd been crying hard. I turned the scope to the woman who had gotten to her feet. Her hands were held loose at her side, and she now was approaching the trembling little girl.

I turned to the barn and saw an old man on a walker make his way into the doorway, the sunlight sparkling off the chromed finish. He was too far away for me to make out his features, but he had to be the grandpa. Laney turned and started running again, her legs pumping in the tall grass, when she suddenly fell, her entire body disappearing in the tall grass.

4

LANEY DIDN'T COME up right away, and the woman's easy walk turned into a fast run. The grandpa stood in the doorway, a hand cupped over his eyes to block out the late afternoon sunlight that must have been blinding him. When two figures rose from the grass that had been disturbed, the woman slid to a stop, a good fifty feet away, a shout of surprise coming out of her mouth. The little girl was struggling as a man in camouflage held her under one arm. She kicked and bit at the arm holding her.

He had a rifle across his back, a boonie hat adorning his head with a small daypack in olive drab in one hand. His belt had pouches and one of them held an old tin GI canteen like the one I wore. He was a good hundred feet from me. I started crawling faster, being less mindful about disturbing things as I got into the tall grass, directly behind the figure.

"Just stop a sec," a male voice grunted as he repositioned the little girl in front of him.

I wanted to drop him where he was, but the woman was closing on him, and he wasn't unarmed. He had a pistol in the left side of his belt, and I could see a strap across his left shoulder and neck, though I didn't see what it was slung to. It must have been in front of his body. Still, I was making good time and all eyes seemed to be on the struggling figures. The woman got there first and started screaming, sobbing, and begging all at the same time. I could barely hear her over the racket the little girl was putting out though. She sounded like a bobcat that was getting skinned alive, with all of it being projected through a bull horn or a college PA speaker set at a ball game.

When I was twenty-five feet away, I rose up. The woman looked over his shoulder at me as I leveled the gun at his back and she fell backward on her butt, screaming for everyone to run. The man took a glance over his shoulder at me, then did a double take. He dropped Laney, who ran to the woman. The little girl launched herself on the ground, into her mother's lap.

"Friend, I mean no harm," the man said, turning, both hands in the air.

His face and exposed skin had been blacked out with grease paint and ashes, though he wore a

33

mosquito face net over his head, under his hat. He had a short-barreled AR slung on a one-point sling in his front. It was odd to me, he was left handed, not something you see every day. I held the rifle up higher, the long silencer almost blocking out my sight picture of his face, and I could see his eyes get as big as saucers.

"Who are you?" he asked me suddenly.

"Get on your knees, and if you go for your guns, it'll be the last thing you'll—"

"Westley?" he asked, pulling his hat off.

"Carter?" I responded in shock.

THE FAMILY HAD FLED BACK INTO THE BARN WHILE WE had our standoff, but now Carter was looking at me angrily.

"You were told to stand down, we'd handle this," he said, exasperated.

"I came here to check things out," I told him. "Jessica and her father didn't seem all that interested in helping." I lowered the rifle to point at the ground between us.

"She said that she told you she would handle it. She called me on the radio, and I'm handling it."

"You bring any food?" I asked him.

"We don't hand out food," told me quietly, his eyes at the ground.

I slung my rifle over my shoulder and adjusted my pack. "I did. And I came to warn them."

"I was here to observe and make contact without alarming them. Looks like I messed that up," he said sheepishly.

I shook my head, not at him so much as the entire situation. I started walking, passing him, pulling the camo netting off my head and letting it fall on top of the tall grass. My goal was the open door that Laney and her mom had disappeared into. I heard Carter follow a few steps later.

"How did you sneak up on me?" he asked.

"I've been hunting my entire life. I didn't see you until you broke cover and stood up. Should have let the little girl keep running and held still," I told him.

"I figured that out after the fact," he said from behind me, his voice thoughtful. "Thought if I had let her go she was going to tear my throat out with her teeth."

I saw a flash of light reflect from the doorway of the barn and saw the edge of the walker. I raised my hands up to show that my hands were empty. A shot rang out and the ground erupted between my feet. I dove down, hearing Carter do the same.

"You're on private property," the old man yelled. "I'll give you thirty seconds to get moving off my land."

"We're here to help," I shouted at the top of my lungs.

The ground erupted next to my head about three feet away. Carter grunted behind me, and I turned to see him wiping chunks of dirt and grass off his face. His boonie hat was hanging by the cords behind his neck and the debris had stuck to the camo paint.

"I said clear out," the old man shouted back.

I was mentally counting down, but rolled on my side, pulling on the straps, shrugging out of my back-pack, leaving my rifle in the grass. I fumbled with the buckle on the pack but got it open. I grabbed a bag of rice and a bag of lentils and stood up slowly, each held above my head. My countdown had gotten to about five seconds when I saw the walker move slowly. Some-body picked it up and shuffled along behind it. I saw the old man come into the light. In one hand, he held the edge of the walker and a rifle. He shuffled a few more steps then stopped and raised the rifle up.

"Don't shoot, I have food for your families," I said, feeling a spot on my chest start to burn.

I knew it was all psychological, but I could almost feel the point of impact if he were to pull the trigger while he considered my words. The rifle wavered, then he lowered it.

"You that fellar who gave my granddaughters the rice 'n' food?"

His voice was loud and clear. I could hear Carter clear his throat, but I beat him to it. "Yes, that was me," I called back.

36

"Come up here slowly," he said. "I may not look like much, but I got you both covered."

"Yes, sir," I called back, my voice not as loud.

I put the food back in the pack, lugged that up, and put the rifle sling across my shoulders. My nerves were on fire from the gunshots, and although my heart was beating faster than I could imagine and my stomach felt like it was going to turn itself inside out, I was starting to calm down. His shots were warning shots, meant to scare us and show that he really had us dead to rights; the same way I had with Carter earlier when I hadn't known who he was. I approached slowly, and Carter caught up with me, walking to my left. We both stopped about twenty feet away.

"You're Bud's grandson," he said, statement, not fact.

"Yes, sir."

"Who are you?" he asked, turning, his rifle now pointing between us, but more or less at the ground.

"Carter, sir, Carter Munising."

The old man's skin was wrinkled, and his face seemed to almost have shriveled in on itself. He was older than my grandparents, by a lot. I wasn't a good judge of age. He was wearing bibs, a long-sleeved flannel shirt, and a green John Deere hat with sweat stains on the brim. A round shape was in his front breast pocket and when he turned and spat a brown stream, I figured he had a dip of Copenhagen or something similar in.

"Looks like this fellar snuck up on you," he said, pointing with the rifle.

"He did, sir. I was watching your farm, working on how to get closer to talk to you when the little girl tripped over my head."

"Laney..." he said, shaking his head. "So, you didn't know each other was coming? You obviously know each other."

"I do, he's a friend of a friend," I told him, keeping my hands relaxed as possible. "But I didn't know he'd be here."

"His girlfriend is like my little sister," Carter told the farmer.

I turned to him, shooting him a puzzled look. Girlfriend?

"Thank you for the food earlier. We're almost out of everything," the old man said. "They're cooking up some now inside. You two aren't with those guys on the motorcycles, are you? You're both dressed like you're playing army."

"No, sir," I said quickly.

Carter shot me a look, then shook his head no also. "I just thought it'd be a good idea to come in unobserved, all things considered."

"What you want to talk to me about?" the farmer asked Carter.

"Probably the same thing he does," he said, using his hand to point at me with his thumb. "The guys on bikes mean to attack the farm, take the..." he stopped, looked around, then spoke quieter, "take the ladies and kids."

"What's that? I'm half deaf."

Carter repeated himself, but louder. The old man's face went pale.

"Mister, who wants to take us and where?" The little voice came out of the darkness, and I saw Mary come out into the light.

She was wearing the same clothing as earlier, but her hair had been brushed out. She was holding a rough teddy bear who was missing an eye, and several stitches had come loose, exposing the stuffing.

"Get back inside," the old man barked, and the child fled like the devil was snapping at her heels. I could hear a murmur of voices in the darkened interior.

"I came to warn you about them and drop off some food. With the kids' fathers being gone—"

"How do you know that?" he asked me sharply.

"Well, they told me that earlier," I said, remembering overhearing the conversation, "and Lance's boys are planning on being back in two days, in force."

"Were you the one who heard that, or were you passing the message along?" Carter asked me suddenly.

"I heard that directly from the two scouts. The guys on bikes. One of them is named Danny."

"I ain't worried about no two or three bikers," the old man said. "Their fathers will straighten things out when they get back," he said, but there was something in his eye that told me he didn't believe that.

"There isn't just two or three of them," I said softly, "and you might want to consider leaving, or going into hiding."

"Son, like I said, when my grandsons get back here—"

"Did your grandsons take off down the road on quads a couple days back?" Carter asked suddenly.

"Yeah, chasing off the pricks who came in last time and tried to steal food out of the corn crib."

"That wasn't a group of thieves, that was Lester," I said quietly, shrugging the pack off.

"Lester? The moonshiner?"

I nodded, not correcting him. Lester was just a cutout, a middle man, the guy everyone went to arrange a shipment of hooch. He didn't make it, he just insulated the people who did. Shared risk and profits. Each of us had our own jobs. "He wasn't trying to steal from you, sir."

"You know this man too?" he asked, turning to Carter. "Where are my boys? Where are my grandsons?"

Carter opened and closed his mouth a few times. I

opened my pack and dumped out the Ziploc bags as quickly as I could and re-shouldered the backpack. I'd left the bags on the ground, but I wanted to be ready. I wasn't prepared to have this conversation. I was still raw myself.

"Where's our husbands?" Laney's mom asked, walking out of the dark, her arm around another woman.

Both were in their early to mid-twenties. Laney's mom was raven haired, whereas the other woman had brownish blondish colored hair. Both wore dirty looking dresses, their hair greasy and dirty, though it was combed and pulled back in loose ponytails.

"They were trying to kill Les," I said. "He fled to our property. They kept shooting at Les trying to kill him..." My words trailed off, I didn't want to say the rest.

The old man's grip on the gun tightened, his knuckles going white with the sudden pressure. His lips pressed together in an angry line as his whole body trembled. A single tear rolled down the side of his face.

"All three of them?" he asked me.

I nodded.

"All three of them what?" the blonde woman asked.

"Dead, my grandsons are dead," the old man said hoarsely, another tear falling from his eye to leave a streak on his cheek.

"I'm sorry, I had no choice," I told them.

"Chasing down a friend of yours?" the blonde woman said, brushing off the raven-haired woman's arm.

"Yes, he's an old man who wouldn't hurt anybody," I answered, noting that Carter was shifting foot to foot, both hands flexing.

I took note of his wary posture and subtle stretching and decided that maybe I wasn't reading this shit storm correctly and saw the furious looks the women were shooting me, rather than the sorrow and resignation the old man was showing.

"How do you know he wasn't with the guys who came by here before, shooting at my son?" Laney's mom hissed.

"That wasn't Les," I said, backing up a step as both women advanced, the old man putting an arm out to symbolically stop them. "I know who probably did it. It's the same group that's coming in two days to take you ladies. The kids too, if the guy called Danny is to be believed."

My words didn't seem to register to them.

"You murdered my husband," the blonde woman hissed and darted forward.

I saw the slap coming and for once I was thankful I didn't have Raider with me. I didn't think he would have allowed her to get close like this with her tone so loud. The sharp blow rang out, turning my head with the force of her fury. I turned back to her, rubbing the side of my cheek. I was fighting off both anger and shame at the same time. The blow had stung and, if she'd been a man, I would have knocked him senseless and stomped his head in. As it was, the woman was probably Linda Carpenter's size, though shorter. She reared back again, and I put my hand up.

"I did not murder your husband," I hissed, my face on fire where I was sure she'd left a handprint. "I stopped him from murdering a friend."

She swung, and I caught her wrist. I squeezed until I could feel the bones grind, which got her attention. She pulled, then tried kicking. I held onto her wrist but backed up, so she had to face me.

"Your husband made his decision. I don't know why he went after our friend, but your husband came onto my property to murder someone else. This is not my fault."

She leaned down to bite at my wrist when nothing else worked. I'd had enough, and before her teeth could sink into my arm, I used my other hand to push on the top of her head, sending her sprawling into Laney's mother. The old man was crying freely now, one hand wiping at his eyes, the other clutching the walker. I watched the woman get to her feet, cursing. Another woman walked into the edge of the opening, the sunlight showing a gaggle of kids behind her. Seven, eight, nine?

"I told them they couldn't try to take stuff from others," she said, her arms around one of the little girls. "They got what I told them would happen."

"And you're ok with that?" the blonde turned and screamed at her. "We're starving here! There's no food, there's barely any water, and don't you think this man hasn't merely killed our husbands, but *all of us* by proxy?"

Her words were sharp, and I realized a half a second too late I could tell her political leanings and education level. I would have been hard-pressed not to have recognized that. In college, I'd met a lot of people like her; politically active and slightly self-entitled. I pointed to the food I'd earlier taken out of my backpack and dropped on the floor in front of me, the old man watching my every move. The blonde woman and the woman who'd just appeared started arguing and bickering, tears flowing freely. They were ignoring the food.

"Let's get out of here," Carter said quietly.

"I did what I could," I said softly, not even to Carter. "I should have let Jessica handle this part," I finished, looking directly at him.

He just nodded at me, and I snapped my pack closed. Grandma had reloaded my backpack with the very basics that I had given away earlier, and I could hear the murmur of the kids behind me. It took everything in my power not to start digging for a candy bar, or some more of Grandma's sourdough bread. Another sharp crack rang out, and I looked up to see the blonde woman had smacked the other. Things were getting ugly, but for right now their attention was not focused on us.

Carter and I were backing away slowly, not making any big moves. Laney's mother had been shouting at the other women who were ready to start pulling hair and scratching eyes out. She'd been in the middle screaming back at both of them with her hand pointing at them in turn when she saw us backing away. She turned and yelled, "And where the hell do you think you're going?"

"I just came to give you the news and some food. I'm sorry for your loss, but you've guys got two days before Lance's group will be coming back." The fighting and bickering stopped when I spoke, but only for a moment.

"How can we trust the guy who murdered our husbands?" the blonde woman asked, her voice high and shrill, her cheeks stained with free-flowing tears.

"You can't trust anyone," Carter told them.

We hadn't stopped moving backward, and now they were advancing on us slowly. I wasn't about to take another slap to the face, but none of them looked armed either. I felt bad about shoving the one woman down on her butt, but I wasn't gonna let her keep escalating, and my cheek burned from more than just guilt and shame; she'd really walloped me a good one. I just hoped they were going to take our warning seriously.

"Who's coming for us?" Laney's mother asked, advancing on us quickly.

"There's a group that's camped out at the Crater of Diamonds. I know at least one of the guys there, Lance, has been up to some pretty nefarious stuff. I overheard two of their men talking. You've got two days and they're going to hit the farm."

"What you mean 'hit the farm'?" Her words were icy, her face a mixture of grief and fury.

"By the sound of things... They're coming here to kill all the men, take the women and any of the children who look interesting to them. If there's any food or anything of use here, they will probably take that too." Carter's words were cold and forceful.

"Kill all the men? Take us? For what?"

"Play toys, barter, currency." Again, Carter's words lacked any sort of warmth.

I could tell when the woman finally understood what it was we'd been trying to get through to her. She was thin from hunger, but her skin tone had a light tan to it. When she realized what we were talking about without overtly saying it in front of the kids, she went pale. If they'd been attacked before, the thought of them dying had probably occurred to them but being raped and traded around as some sort of sexual slaves obviously hadn't. Add that to the fact the kids appeared to be at least on someone's wish list... I felt sick even thinking about it. I could say without a doubt that there would be one man I would have no qualms or nightmares about killing: the guy on the bike named Danny. Even his partner had been disgusted with him.

"And we've got two days?" she asked over the screaming, wailing, and carrying on of the kids, the crying of the grandpa, and the two women who'd gone back to yelling at the kids and not each other.

"I heard it from their own lips. Blue team did another slow drive by and then they were told to head back to base and rest up, because in two days' time they were hitting the farm here."

"Blue team?" Carter asked me.

"I'll tell you later," I said to him softly. "We need to talk to Jessica."

"Yeah, we do," he murmured, and I almost didn't catch his words.

"What should we do?" she asked us.

"Get out of here, take everything you guys can and leave," I told her.

"I'll talk to my father-in-law," she said quietly, then turned and started screaming at the woman who'd walloped me.

It was a good time to get going.

5

CARTER and I walked away from the mess I'd made. At least I knew now, from the one woman's words and actions, that the men hadn't necessarily been on the up and up. It weighed heavily on my mind. No one wanted to see a kid be hungry or starve. But how much was enough? I'd given them food that would probably last them awhile. If they were smart they'd take that food and get out of the area. Somehow, I didn't think they would though; I wasn't sure if they even could.

Carter and I had backed out as far away from them as we could and started down the road toward my grandparents' house. We wanted to make sure we were far out of sight, out of earshot. I knew the grandpa had a gun, but the women were so upset with us that I was half convinced I was going to get a bullet in the back if I would've turned when I walked away. I didn't tell

Carter about the bike that I had stashed; instead, we went across the street and up the slope a ways and sat under an old tree. There was a hollowed-out spot in the tall grass where deer or something else had bedded down, and with a start I realized this could've been one of the places the bikers had used to spy on the farm.

"You shouldn't have gone there," Carter scolded me.

"They had no food, and I'm responsible for killing at least one of them. Hell, I know for sure I killed one of them, you guys got the other ones. It didn't feel right, when I didn't know the entire story, to just leave them alone. I wanted to give them some food, at least give them the warning in person."

"That was part of my plan. I've been out here or near the Crater of Diamonds since we left your place. I got the call on the radio, hell I heard your call to Jess. As soon as you got off the horn I switched frequencies and got my marching orders from Linda." Carter swatted at a mosquito that was trying to land on his face.

I didn't know how it had gotten so late so fast, but I realized that dusk was coming. In the summer time the days were long and hot. The passing of time like this normally wouldn't have been missed by me, but it had been an emotional and taxing day. I was ready for it to be over with, and I didn't want to hear any more scolding from Jessica's group.

"What are you guys going to do about the raiders who are coming?" I asked him after a while.

Carter sat down next to me and shrugged his daypack off his shoulders. Next, he laid his carbine down across the pack, mindful to keep the barrel out of the dirt. He stretched and then pulled a canteen out, unscrewed the top, and took a long drink. I waited.

"I don't know," he said after a while. "We don't have the manpower to fight off everyone from the crater gang. We literally don't have enough people."

"The Hillbilly Mafia," I said softly. "It's only fitting since most of them are rednecks and hillbillies."

Carter grunted and pulled a protein bar out of a pouch on the right side of his belt. "Want one?" he asked, offering it up.

"No thanks," I pulled my pack to me and took out the other half of sourdough Grandma had sent with me, when she'd reloaded my pack sometime when I wasn't paying attention. I offered him a piece and he broke off a chunk and started chewing it. His eyes got big as its flavor hit his mouth, and he washed it down with water. We sat in silence for a while and considered our options.

"The only thing we can do is hope that they take our warning and get out of there."

I looked at Carter, nodding, but wishing there was more that could be done.

"Do you have any idea what time they were talking about coming?" Carter asked quietly.

"Do I know when they're planning to attack? No, no I don't. I wish I did, but I don't even think Lance is in charge anymore."

Carter finished off the chunk of sourdough I'd given him and washed it down with water. I dug in myself, being used to eating simple foods like this. Flour, water, sourdough starter; just add heat and you have a simple bread. And sourdough starter wasn't anything special to begin with; you just kept it fed and growing with flour and water. It was simple food that people had been making for hundreds if not thousands of years.

"What I think you're seeming to forget here is that it doesn't matter who's in charge over there. We know for sure that they've killed close to ten people now and kidnapped more. We've been keeping an eye on them. I really think the only chance those women and kids have is to get out of there and go into hiding."

He was right, and I knew he was right. But what if they didn't go? Could I live with myself? I was thinking about all of this when Carter put a hand up to his left ear and cocked his head to the side. I hadn't noticed it before, but he'd put in an earwig and it must've been attached to the radio on his vest. I couldn't hear what was said to him, but he spoke into the radio softly.

"... Westley? He's here with me. Yeah, he went back

to bring them some food. No, no they were all in pretty rough shape. They don't look like they've had a solid meal in weeks. No, there were no problems getting out of there. Yeah, the gunshots our scouts heard were the farmer letting us know he had us in sight. No, they weren't hostile, and they didn't try to hurt us. Yeah, I would say Westley is pissed. That ain't my problem, Jessica, you talk to them. Okay, see you back there. Carter out."

"Well, what did she have to say?" I asked him.

"Other than the fact that you're a dumbass? Nothing much. She just wanted to know if I'd made contact, because she hadn't been able to get you and your grandparents on the radio."

"That's because I got the radio on me, and when I was doing my stalk, I had it turned off so wouldn't give away my position."

"Someday I want to ask you about that, how you got so good. Sneaking up on me like that?"

"Lots of years getting squirrel and deer out of season."

"That's why you got that little varmint rifle then?" He tapped the can on the end of the barrel.

"Yeah, it doesn't make a lot of sound, but most of the time it was other things like trapping. Making snares, only using the gun if I had to put something down, or I was in a spot where I could shoot without the shot being heard. Speaking of shots... scouts?" I asked.

"We've had this entire area being watched. When they heard the farmer trying to scare us with those shots, they radioed it back in along with the general direction."

WE'D TALKED AND WAITED AWHILE BEFORE HE GOT another message on the radio and motioned for me to follow. We'd stopped talking, with nothing much to say. He was of the opinion that we'd done all we could to help the families by giving them enough food for now and warning them to get out of the area. I wasn't happy with that, and I wished I had my buddy Raider here with me. More than likely, he'd know what to do. Lord knows I didn't. My brain said I'd done enough, but my heart didn't agree.

I didn't ask where we were going, but saw we were more or less moving north and west. We'd left the main road and had been moving cross country, first through some brush, then into a thinly wooded area I was familiar with. I saw old landmarks, places I'd hunted before, like a small creek that always had been good for taking frogs and turtles but never had any fish. We stopped in a spot I'd once taken a deer, and I hunkered down next to Carter.

"What are we doing?" I asked him quietly.

"We're waiting for somebody," he said cryptically.

"Who?" I wanted to know.

He didn't say anything, but instead looked over my shoulder. I turned and saw a figure in camo come out of the brush behind us by about twenty feet. I shouldered the rifle without thinking about it when Carter gently pushed the barrel down.

"Jess."

I lowered the rifle's barrel, but kept it shouldered. I watched as the figure walked closer and then it took off the boonie hat, her hair flowing free as she shook her head. It looked both scripted and unconscious at the same time.

"Wes," she said, walking up to me, her carbine held low and to the ready.

"Jessica," I said, tipping an imaginary hat.

"Ma'am," Carter said, "think I'll head back to my spot."

"Take care," Jess said quietly, not even watching him leave.

I was suddenly so pissed at her, at myself, at the world. My emotions were all over the board. She hadn't sounded like she was going to help them, but half a day later, as the sun was setting, here she was!

"What are you doing out here?" I asked her suddenly, my voice cross.

"Told you we would handle it," she said, her voice just as angry as mine.

"Sure, didn't sound like you were planning on doing anything," I shot back.

"We were on unsecured radios, where anybody who could dial into the frequency could have listened in. The chances of that happening were slim but..."

I felt stupid. She was right; what else was she going to say over the open air? The radios looked fancier than CB radios, and I'd forgotten we probably weren't the only ones in the world who had them. Stupid! I kicked myself.

"I... You're right," I agreed.

"I know I am, and if you learn that now, you'll go a lot farther in life," she said with a grin.

It was infectious, and despite the residual anger and tension, I let out a small chuckle myself.

"It's going to be dark soon," she pointed out.

"I have to get back to the farm, figure something out—"

"We don't have enough people to do anything if they decide to hit the farm, and the family hasn't left. The crater gang is close to seventy people now, with more coming in daily."

"What if we snuck in there and attacked first? Like when you got the Guthries out?" I asked her.

She was already shaking her head. "We don't know

how many of them are innocent. There are people coming and going, but mostly coming in. They've killed several of their own in various squabbles, but they've been shooting some of the people they've taken hostage."

"Taken hostage?"

"Like our mutual friends, they believe some of these folks hid back from the government and have a stash of food."

"So, they're just..."

"Yes," she said softly.

"I didn't leave the radio with my grandparents, so I need to get back tonight," I said suddenly.

"I'll come with you." She spoke into her own radio softly, nodding at whatever they were saying.

"I have to find my bike before it gets too dark."

"Ok, let's do that then. Road is directly south of us," she said, looking at a compass.

"I know where we are," I told her. "Spent most of my youth up and down this patch. We're actually on the Crater of Diamond's land right here."

"But..." she said, her words trailing off as we heard the sound of a gunshot in the distance.

I turned and followed the direction I'd heard it come from. The farm. I waited, tensing, praying they weren't starting the attack tonight. We were waiting in silence when I felt Jessica's hand take mine. Her hand was rough, calloused, and small. Like it was made to fit right there.

"I think we're safe to go," she said, breaking the silence.

———

WE FOUND MY BIKE RIGHT WHERE I'D STASHED IT, AND I walked it back with her. Both of us had probably come to the same conclusion that we couldn't ride double on it. There wasn't any room and with my pack and my weight, it was almost enough to pancake the tires. Besides the fact was no room to actually fit both of us made it almost a no-brainer.

"So, have you thought about trading our group some of that moonshine?" Jessica asked me suddenly, the light of day almost gone.

"Here I am worried about somebody else's kids getting snatched by bad people, and you're wanting to talk about getting liquored up?" I teased.

"One of the big problems we have is that some of our vehicles are gas powered. We tried to get more as the troops showed up, but we couldn't. Resources were federalized. Once we bugged out, we realized that water must have gotten into our gas storage tanks. We've gotten some of our vehicles working again, but..."

"You used regular unleaded when you got your fuel stores setup?" I asked her.

"Yes, we didn't want to raise suspicions by buying in

bulk and having a tanker deliver gasoline to an old clear cut on forestry land."

"Ahhh, I actually meant, you got the stuff with ethanol in it?"

"Yes?" she said, her voice uncertain.

"That doesn't store as well. The additives in it remain good for a while, but ethanol itself attracts and absorbs water," I avoided lingo I knew from college. "So, if you had it stored for more than a year without adding something like Stabil in it, it might have pulled moisture out of the air every time you filled a drum."

"I... We did use some Stabil in each drum, but... I guess that makes sense. We could never figure out how water got in."

"Lots of useless things I learned in college," I told her truthfully. "A degree in chemistry makes me a better moonshiner."

"Chemistry," she mused, "like the art of making things go boom?" she asked, using her hands to mime a big explosion.

"Most of the time, we take precautions to keep everything we're doing from catching fire or..." I let my words trail off.

Two days... we had two days. Less now, after today. Not nearly enough.

"I hope they decide to leave," I told her.

"They have to, we can't protect them." Her words

were soft, but I could tell her mind was already made up; mine wasn't.

A bark had both of us looking up the slope. A figure ghosted out of the edge of the darkness and a canine came to a rest next to him, tail wagging so hard his rear end was nearly bouncing.

"Grandpa?" I asked.

"No, it's the lollypop guild, here to get yer dues," he shot back.

Raider lurched forward when he heard my voice and put his front paws on me. I pushed him back a little bit, then hugged him close. My face got a quick wash down from my happy dog before I backed up, forcing him to go down to his feet.

"Your grandma was worried about you when I left a couple hours ago. We heard a few rifle shots but wasn't sure if it was from your direction."

"It was," I confirmed. "Two when Carter and I were there at the farm, and one later on, after I'd met up with Jessica."

"Ma'am," Grandpa said, tilting an imaginary hat, "almost didn't see you there."

"Am I really that hard to miss?" she asked.

"No," he said shortly and turned. "Lights are on inside, and your grandma has boiling water... just in case."

"Nobody's hurt," I assured him.

He stopped and turned to me, his hand reaching out to my chin, turning my head.

"Moonlight here sucks," he said, looking up at the tree cover, "but it looks like you got yourself some spousal correction, if the bruise looks about right."

"Spousal correction?" Jessica asked, an eyebrow arched.

"Yeah, it's what his grandma tells me when I do something stupid and she backhands me. Come on, we got food ready at home. I don't think she'll mind so much if you decide to stay for supper."

"She can have my room tonight," I said.

Raider whined and rubbed his head against my thigh, pushing me a little bit away from Jess. Grandpa laughed slowly at the dog's antics and kept pace with us.

"Where two grown assed adults sleep is none of my business. I'm half deaf anyway," Grandpa groused.

My ears burned in the dark, and Jessica took my hand. I saw her grinning, teeth showing. I rolled my eyes and Grandpa laughed a little louder, reaching across her and smacking me on the shoulder.

6

GRANDPA CHANGED out of his homemade ghillie suit while we tucked into the food. Grandma came out once to kiss me on the forehead, then scurried off. It wasn't like her and Grandpa to make themselves scarce so quickly. They loved to talk as much as anybody. In fact, I think they did it, so we could have some alone time. We both avoided talking about what happened at the farm today. I knew I was thinking things over and praying that the families moved on.

"See, our first date went rather well," Jessica said, pushing her plate back.

"Our first date?" I asked her.

"A candlelit dinner, some drinks," she said, pointing to the pitcher of Grandma's doctored lemonade, "a walk down a country road together..." she said it wistfully, and I snorted.

Baked beans, rice covered with some home canned venison in brown gravy, a wedge of cornbread and some hooch that I'd made in the barn. I wasn't sure how to take things, especially with her. She was right about the candles; we'd used those instead of the alcohol lamps.

"Sorry our first date couldn't be… fancier."

"Come on," she said, taking my hand and pulling me to my feet.

Raider had been snoozing under the table, but as soon as my chair moved, he shot upright and was sniffing at both of us as Jess grabbed our glasses and shooed me out onto the front porch. She indicated my chair, and I took it. She sat in Grandma's, right next to me. Raider looked uncertain, then jumped up onto the rocker Grandpa loved. He wobbled a bit, then turned in the chair before sitting down, watching us.

"There will be no shenanigans," I said, pointing at him.

"Is that a statement or question?" Jessica asked out of the darkness.

"You like watching me turn red all of a sudden," I said, changing the subject subtly.

"No, I just… Oh hell. I was a tomboy growing up, then I joined the military where it's mainly the men's club. When I'm with you… I am just me, and you always treat me like a lady, not like one of the guys."

"You are a lady."

"That's why I like you," she told me, getting up.

I was about to take a sip, but she pulled my cup out of my hand and set it on the rail behind me, putting hers beside it. I watched, wondering if I'd somehow screwed things up. She turned and straddled me, then pulled me in tight. The kiss set off fireworks inside my head and heart. Raider whined in the background, annoyed, but I ignored him. I was grimy, smelly, sweaty, yet she was softly pulling at my shirt. I found my hands making similar tugs at her clothing as well as the kiss deepened, changed.

"The barn?" she asked me, panting, her voice hoarse and excited.

We could lay out our clothes in the shine room. It was the cleanest of all the barn. A bale or two of hay with our clothing over the top... Her shirt now untucked, I started on the buttons. She pulled mine over my head between kisses, her hand reaching down to my inner thigh. I couldn't help but groan as she started moving her hand up.

"Yes," I said, gasping as her teeth bit into my neck.

I stood, scooping her up in my arms, her shirt falling open. "Raider, stay here, stay watch," I told him.

Raider laid down in the chair, putting both paws over his snout as I carried Jessica into the barn. It was dark, but when I got to the shine room I turned on the light. The battery-powered LEDs came on. We both squinted, and I put her down. She finished removing her shirt, tossing it on top of the hay bale we used against the back of the stall for a table, and turned away from me. She snaked one hand up and undid the catch on her bra, letting it fall to the floor.

My mouth was dry. We wouldn't need the clothes after all, the old moving blanket I'd washed before the power went out was still in there, folded neatly. I had planned on letting Raider use it as a bed while we ran shine, but there it sat, forgotten. Jessica turned to face me.

"Turn off the light," she said.

THE SUN SEEMED TO BE SEARING MY EYES THROUGH MY eyelids. I woke up, my arms and legs intertwined with... Jessica! I remembered the night before now as the cobwebs cleared from my brain. I tried to untangle myself, but she cuddled in harder, pressing her nude form tight against me. That did all sorts of things to the suddenly raging hormones I thought I'd quieted a decade earlier and pulled off half the blanket we'd used to cover up.

She pulled me tighter, burying her head in the crook of my neck. "Not yet," she said quietly.

I wasn't about to argue and covered us back up. She kissed my neck, then my jawline. My body shivered at the pleasure, both remembered and yet to come, when

I heard the barn's main door open slightly and pawed footsteps running to the closed stall door, then sniffing.

"Raider, go away," I said quietly.

"You in here?" Grandma called out.

"Oh shit," Jessica said and pulled the covers over her head just as the door to the stall opened.

Our arms and legs were sticking out, but I managed to pull the covers down, so I could see out without uncovering anything important.

"Grandma..."

"It's about damned time," she said, then left, slamming the stall door behind her. "Come on, Raider, time to get eggs, and if you give my baby anymore guff, I'll feed your carcass to Foghorn."

"Did she really just..." Jessica said, giggling.

"I think so?" I said.

A tone went off near Jessica's pile of clothes. She pushed the covers off and untangled herself from me, shooting me a smile over her shoulder. I watched her as she picked through things and found her radio. She put the ear piece in and then spoke.

"Jessica here. Yeah, sure did. No, not that we can figure. If they don't, it's on them. I know, but there's at least seventy-five at the camp. No. That hasn't changed, has it?"

I watched, almost lost for words. It had been mostly dark last night. I'd gotten a glimpse of her before the lights went out and as our eyes had readjusted to the dark, but now I had sunlight spilling in through slots between the beams and I could make her out clearly.

"Keep me posted. Yeah, good idea. Yager and Diesel will work. No, don't. Mom doesn't need to. Dad, listen here..." I grinned at hearing those words, she had let out a big sigh.

"...No, I stayed the night. The couch? No, I slept in the barn. Oh, he offered me his bed all right," she said, shooting me a grin.

I felt like a giant target had just been painted on my back.

"...Yeah, Dad. No, everything is good here. We need to add another spotter near the camp, so we can see when they roll out tomorrow. Yeah. Need to make sure we're ready in case the farm is a diversion. We can't let them surprise us again."

I listened in shock, but her side of the conversation was all I could hear. Or was it? I looked around for my clothes and started putting them on. Had I left the radio in my pack, or was it clipped to my pants? Was she telling her dad what was happening? It could go either way by her words. It was maddening. Then I thought of her dad, and my blood ran cold. If he knew, would he care? I shook my head, pulling my jeans on. The radio wasn't here. I pulled my socks and then boots on, sitting in the old ottoman on the other side of the room as Jessica walked around, finding her clothing.

She put the radio down and turned to me, a bundle of clothing in her arms. "Time to work."

I looked at her standing naked, looking at me hungrily, but knew she was right, "You going to fill me in on the plan?" I asked her.

She started dressing, and I could hardly look away, but I couldn't find my shirt.

"The plan is to watch Lance's gang. I guess ten more came in last night."

"More hostages?" I asked her, shocked.

"No, more men on Harleys. There's some kind of search going on, but our scouts have been able to stay hidden. Their men aren't very good so far."

"I forgot to tell you over the radio," I started, "Marshall, his little cousin?"

"Yeah, barely nineteen? Skinny kid?"

"Yeah, that's him. The guys on bikes mentioned that the boss was looking for him, and not to let Lance find out they lost him."

"Who is the boss?" she asked me seriously.

It was hard to be serious right now, so I closed my eyes a second, so I could focus on her question. What was it again?

"I don't know," I answered, "but I'm willing to guess he's with the bikers I saw."

"Military?"

"I don't know. They were part of 'Blue Team', whatever that is."

She finished and walked over, lightly slapping me on the chin playfully, then used her hand to push my chin aside. She laid her hand across the sore side of my face, her eyes narrowing. "Which of the ladies hit you?"

"I think it was Laney's mom. A blondish lady, why?"

"Because I want to scratch her eyes out after I punch her in the boob and bust her kneecaps," she said, rubbing the bruise.

"First date then a roll in the hay, and you're already wanting to defend my honor?" I asked her, teasing.

"That's just a start. That's how girls fight dirty. I can fight like a man too."

"I believe you," I told her, opening the stall door, "and I like it. But... let's make sure they get out of there first. I don't—"

"Let's get cleaned up a bit, and we'll talk more. Maybe I'll head out there with you, and we can see if we can talk them into getting out if they haven't already?"

"I'd like that."

Grandma, Grandpa, and Raider were just outside the barn's roll-away door. They were too far away to have heard anything, but they were waiting. At least Grandpa and Raider were; Grandma had the chickens all around her feet as she spread scratch feed from her coffee can.

"I heated four pots of water for your bath," Grandma said without turning to us when we walked up.

"Thank you," I told her.

"Wasn't for you, it's for Miss Jessica," Grandpa said, turning and shooting me a grin.

"Pigs waller a bit, they get hosed off outside. I expect a couple buckets of cold water would do you good," Grandma told me with a snort, finally turning.

Jessica and I both chuckled, and she gave me a playful shove as she jogged to the house.

"Let's see your face in the light," Grandma said.

I let her look, brushing chaff off my arms as she turned my head side to side. "Your woman do that to you?"

"You didn't notice it last night?" I asked her.

"Somebody else walloped you?" Grandma asked.

I nodded. "One of the kid's mothers. You sure didn't stick around long last night. You feeling ok?"

"I saw the way you were looking at each other. I figured a couple stiff drinks, some cotton in my ears... then this morning your bed was still made, and you were nowhere to be found."

"I... well..."

"At least you had the good sense to clean up after

yourself after dinner," Grandma said, then turned and followed Jess into the house.

"I didn't do the dishes..." I said, my words trailing off as Grandpa held a finger over his lips until Grandma was out of earshot, then he held out a hand.

Confused, I shook with him, watching Raider's tail start wagging.

"I did. I waited until I knew the shenanigans wasn't going to happen on the front table or porch. When I heard the barn door open, I snuck out and did 'em up. Your grandma's pretending to be grumpy, but when she saw Jessica coming down the driveway with you, she told me she was happy for you."

"She didn't exactly come to the house to, uh..."

"Oh, I know, I know," he said a little too quickly.

We turned to the porch and I saw something hanging over the rails. My shirt! I reached over and took it.

"Well, the porch was *almost* shenanigan free," I said ruefully.

"Buckets are by the hand pump." He grinned as he said it. "And don't drop the soap; the chickens are likely to nibble on any hanging bits."

"Come on!" I protested, finally getting frustrated.

He just cackled.

7

I WAS SORE in places I hadn't been sore in for a long time. Walking with Jessica was helping work those kinks out though. I wore plain clothing, and she'd had a change of essentials in her pack as well. When she'd come out of the bathroom wearing one of my button-up shirts, I'd about fell out of the chair, but Grandma and she had somehow colluded. I didn't know what it was about, but I was sure it was nefarious. Seeing her in my shirt had my heart doing all sort of flip flops. We'd decided to walk up together, though not unarmed. We'd come in the way I had, but as soon as we saw things were safe, we'd approach openly.

We figured a man and a woman, even armed, wouldn't be as intimidating as two men in camouflage, like Carter and I had the other day. We had our packs and rifles, she had a pistol on her belt as well, but she had claimed my white cotton button-up for herself and had the front edges tied, showing her flat, tanned stomach, with the sleeves rolled up. Grandma and she had fussed with her hair, and in the end, she had given Jessica a straw cowboy hat from her own collection. It was old, worn, but it looked fantastic on her.

This time we'd taken Raider.

He barked once, sharply, when he saw the area where I'd first hidden with him. I shushed him and pointed out the lay of the land; where I'd first seen the girls, where Carter and I had figured out where each other was. Without breaking cover, I pointed out the landmarks while she used field glasses to look around. When she was happy that the place wasn't being attacked, we went out into the open.

We talked about the camo, but her wearing a bright white shirt was deliberate. After yesterday, people were going to be jumpy. They might also be really angry, which would make her an extremely easy target to find. With no way to gauge their moods, we approached, but from the tree line cutting through the field as I had done before. I saw a flash of movement and pointed. A face peeked out from behind a tree almost thirty feet away.

"Mary?" I asked the little girl who walked out into the open toward us.

"I'm Laney, Mary is my cousin," she said. "Can I have another candy bar?"

"You remember me from yesterday?" I asked, handing my rifle to Jessica so I could get my pack off.

"Yeah, the little boys aren't crying because their tummies hurt. You brought more food after the first two foods you gave us," she said.

She was cute, not very old, but I could see the lines of hunger had aged her, made her a little more... mature? I pulled my pack off and dug into a side pocket. I found the candy bar I'd packed as a just in case. Her eyes went big as she saw it, then her smile disappeared.

"What's wrong, honey?" Jessica asked her, putting my pack down and taking a knee.

"There's only one. My brothers didn't get candy and I did, yesterday. I can't take it."

"Then take it for your brothers, give it to them," I told her.

She bit her lip then nodded and took it from me like it was the most precious thing on earth.

"Are your moms still mad at us?" I asked her.

"My momma cried herself to sleep. She seems better today, but we're busy packing."

"So, you guys are leaving?" I asked her, relieved.

"Yes, Mary's momma said there are bad men coming to take us, and we need to go and hide. That's why when I saw you two coming I hid. Then I saw it was you, and you gave me chocolate when I really needed it."

Her words were solemn, but they choked me up a bit. Raider must have sensed it because he grumbled, then sat at my feet, looking from her to us.

"Your families are all leaving today?" I asked her.

"I think so. I'm sorry your face hurts," she said, changing the subject suddenly. "My momma was having an 'episode'. Aunt Emily says, she shouldn't have hit you. Does it hurt?"

I knelt and started digging in my pack. Laney walked up and touched my face, startling me.

"It hurts, just a little bit," I said, hoping the hard candies I'd packed for emergency energy were still in there.

"It hurts me just to look at your face," she said seriously.

Jessica snorted, and being the mature individual that I was, I flipped her off behind the girl's back. Laney turned to see what I was doing, but Jess had resorted to gnawing on a fist, my rifle cradled in her other arm, butt on the ground.

"Should we talk to your moms and grandpa?" I asked her.

"Please don't," Laney said just as I found the candy, "I don't want Mom to cry that hard anymore. She's not on her medicines, and she's not nice when she's not on her medicines."

I pulled the candy out and gave her a large handful out of the baggie I kept for emergencies. Her eyes got wide, then she looked at me and her eyes narrowed. It wasn't poisoned; in fact, I used it for a quick burst of energy. Same reason I kept things like caffeine tablets from the dollar store in my prepping supplies. It just plain worked.

"Why are you being nice to us?"

Jessica stood up and turned, facing the barn.

"I..."

"I know what happened to my daddy," she said, looking at the ground, her hand still on my cheek. "I heard him talking to my uncles about using their guns to scare people into giving them food. You're just giving us food. We didn't even scare you." Her eyes were piercing as she met my gaze.

"Does anybody need a reason to be nice and compassionate to some kids who looked like they needed chocolate?" I asked her.

She'd opened her mouth to answer, when I saw two figures step out of the tree line. It was two of the moms, Laney's mother, and the one who'd come out last, yesterday.

"Laney," she said, her voice even, "you can't take off like that, with us getting ready to leave."

"I thought I saw someone, and I did," she said, her voice carrying.

Both women had seen us, and either I was recognized, or we were deemed to not be a threat. Either or was fine with me as long as it kept us out of Grandpa's crosshairs. He'd proven yesterday that, walker or not, he was a fair shot.

"Come back to—"

The smaller woman poked Laney's mother with her elbow, and they both came to a stop in front of us. Both wore men's shirts and had their hair severely tied back under old ball caps probably belonging to the farmer. They eyeballed Jessica and I, and Raider eyeballed everyone, especially the food in the little girl's hands.

"I just came here to check in. My name's Wes, this is my girlfriend Jessica. We've been tracking the group and wanted to see..."

"If we're still here or pushing up daisies?" the bitter woman asked, but most of the fight was out of her.

"Mom, what's pushing up daisies mean?" Laney asked.

The other woman rolled her eyes. "Thank you for checking on us. We're taking your advice, we have a place we can go to today. We have to wheel Grandpa in one of the wheelbarrows, but the older boys and girls have been moving stuff already."

"I... I was just checking. I feel horrible about—"

Laney's mother raised her hand as if to slap me. I thought Raider and Jessica were about to erupt when she changed her mind and put her hands over her face. Silent sobs started wracking her and Laney dropped some candy, trying to shove it in her pockets so she could run to her mom's side. I watched a moment.

"We all knew what our husbands had done and were doing. I guess it makes us guilty as well," the woman I guessed to be Aunt Emily said, "but it's hard to feel guilty when our kids are crying, their bellies are empty, and there's all this terrifying loneliness, not being sure who's going to come back, if ever. Our kids risk their lives every day to try to pick enough berries and fruit for themselves. We don't want them to, but we've all been forced to do it. There's not enough food to go around. It's hard to feel guilty about accepting the fact our husbands are dead and we told them they shouldn't do it, but we let them anyway."

"I feel horrible about things," I said simply, "I just want to make sure you guys get out, and as soon as possible. Things aren't safe around here anymore."

The crying woman dropped her hands and wiped her face. "I'm sorry for hitting you," she said softly.

"I'm sorry. For everything," I told her, meaning it.

The power outage, her husband, how they'd had to adjust their morals to even be able to feed their kids. What I didn't say was that I wasn't sorry that I now felt a little number. I'd gotten the... what was the word? Closure? I felt a little better about things, despite her tears.

Raider barked then got to his feet, nosing the dropped candies. Laney saw that and shrieked once.

She had since pocketed the remaining candy and jumped on the ground like a soldier covering a grenade to save his teammates from shrapnel. Raider gave her a doggy grin, then put his nose by her ear, licking the side of her face.

"He looks like Boppy, but bigger," Laney said as she got to her feet.

The name had Raider turning his head to the side, considering the girl.

"He does a bit," her mom said with a sniff, "but your dad said Boppy got hit by a car, remember?"

The three of them choked up at once, and I closed my pack and put it back on my shoulders. Jessica handed me the rifle. Laney nodded to her mom, a tear falling down her face. I was watching Raider, who was suddenly taking a new interest in the little girl.

"We need to coordinate things with our families after everything settles down," Jessica said, looking at the farmland and the barn.

"What do you mean?" Emily asked.

"Do you have the fuel and help needed to run the farm the way it should?"

"Not anymore," the other one said in a hoarse whisper.

"We can help. Do you guys have radios?"

The ladies shook their heads. Jessica handed me her rifle this time, and she dug in her own pack. She pulled out a Baofeng, like the one I had been given.

"This one has two frequencies programmed in as one and two. Check it off and on, once things cool down here, our group will be in touch. Maybe we can help each other out? In the meantime, the gang that's coming here... it's way too big for us to handle. For anybody to handle."

"I wish we could just blow them all up," Laney said suddenly.

Jessica looked at me, and I knew she had an idea.

"Me too kid," I told her.

"We have to go. We'll see you two later," Jessica said, and took her rifle back from me.

"Thank you," Emily called over our shoulders.

I waved, too numb from the conversation.

"Now what?" I asked Jessica after we'd gone a mile down the road.

She pointed to a spot under a tree where the tall grass was. "Strip."

"Wait, what?"

"Time to get our camo on."

I was disappointed, but it was part two of her plan. She stripped off my shirt she had stolen from my dresser and had a lightweight camo pullover covering her up before I could even get a double take. I pulled my pack off and got my camo netting out. There was still enough color in the summertime that my usual clothing wouldn't give me away with the netting on. I started pulling handfuls of long grass, snapped some green saplings, and started weaving them through the netting.

She looked at me and nodded, then we settled down in the shade. My canteen was in my pack instead of my belt, along with a thermos of hand-pumped well water. I hoped it would stay cool long enough. We sat back and waited for her radio. Raider sat next to me, though I could tell he was restless. I wanted him more for his senses than his attack dog nature. I hoped I wouldn't need it.

———

At some point I dozed. The heat of the day had come and gone. Now, it was starting to get merely muggy and not horrible. Jess was stretched out next to me, laying on her stomach, her field glasses in front of her, and a notebook with some numbers scratched on it, but no Raider.

"Jess," I whispered.

She turned and shot me a grin. She'd crawled under the netting herself, getting into the shade. One end was propped up with some broken sticks making an opening we could see out of, but it would be difficult to make us out unless you walked right up on us.

"Where's my dog?" I asked her.

"Raider," Jess whispered.

"Yeah, where's my..." my words trailed off as a small form stood up and stretched on the other side of her.

"I think he likes me," she whispered back.

The dog had crawled to her side somehow and had been lying flat next to her. I hadn't even seen him he'd been holding so still.

"I think so too. Anything?" I asked her.

"No," she whispered back. "The scouts said the family took off in a large group, heading toward the back of the property where they lost them."

"Good, I'm glad they got out of there. Now we just have to make sure when the Hillbilly Mafia comes, they leave the area good and disgusted. Hopefully without burning the place down."

"Couldn't stop them even if we tried," Jess whispered back.

Part two of the plan was simple: watch, observe, be one set of eyes. Make sure the families got out today. The actual farm was going to be watched by a team of men whom I'd never met, and Jess hadn't volunteered names. We were on the outer edges of the rough semi-circular perimeter of the area being watched, with the crater at one end. Jess' group must have some significant fears about Lance's group if they were actively spending man power to watch what was going on. Even if the cops were around, they would also be outmanned and outgunned according to what I'd learned. We hoped to see them off safely and avoid any advance scouts that Lance's crew was bringing in ahead of schedule. It seemed like the smart thing to do, so we had decided after we'd spoken with the ladies and confirmed that they were going to leave, that we'd sit and wait to make sure they had.

That way, if there were eyes there that Jess' scouts had missed, they might be forced to split and follow the family or us. The camp at the crater had grown, but her group hadn't known that Marshall was gone. Had a quiet coup gone down using Lance's family as leverage? The kid seemed stupid to me, but not a killer. A small part of me hoped he'd got away from those assholes safely. If he was guilty of anything from what little I'd seen of him, it was terminal stupidity coupled with a healthy curiosity. I remembered having had him at shotgun point before. There wasn't a lot of guile in the kid, but I hadn't understood why Lance was so protective of him. But even that didn't change the fact that Lance had kidnapped, tortured, and had people murdered. He'd get his day.

The day had grown long, and I'd pulled out some food I'd packed in for Raider. He was hungrily eating it out of a pie tin I used in place of a pan to cook in. I wasn't planning on cooking in it today or tomorrow anyway. We were waiting, watching and, if possible, following. With the farmer's family bugging out, Lance's crew would be hitting an empty homestead. They had all been gone for hours now, according to the handful of people a lot closer than us.

I was worried what would happen if the Hill-billy Mafia decided to go hit our place next, but we'd done pretty good to make it look like we were empty. That's why Jess and I were the furthest ones away and spitting distance from home. If they drove past us, it was a quick run back to our homestead, and Jess and Grandma had outlined the plan. None of that was good enough, until Jess all but told me that Carter and Jimmy were watching our place. Half of me wondered if the both of us with Raider should have been at the farm instead of here, but then we wouldn't have time alone.

"So how much longer do you want to wait until we head back to the farm?" I asked her, our main mission done.

"Let's wait for dusk, maybe another twenty minutes?"

"Sounds good to me," I said.

Raider chuffed in amusement and got up to stretch. Jess held the camo netting open and told him to go use the potty. I grinned at her choice of words. She had guys named Yager and Diesel, but... potty? I decided to keep the humor to myself. Raider darted out from under the netting and picked a tree a good twenty feet back from our hide to do his deed. We waited. Jess was going to head back to the house with me, and we were going to relieve Carter and Jimmy, so they could watch the Crater crew.

"Here he comes," Jess said as Raider came trotting back.

He stopped at the netting, sniffed, then chuffed and laid down in front of us.

"Come on in, boy," I said, patting the spot on my side.

Instead, he put his nose between us and pushed his way through. Jess and I scooted a bit to make room, then Jess stiffened and rolled to her side, giving the dog a lot of room. She held a hand over her ear and pressed the PTT button on her shirt.

"Go ahead, Carter. Yeah? Jimmy did? You weren't supposed... Uh huh. Ok, I don't like it, but she's the expert. They did what? Ok, we're going to hunker and wait longer then. Ok, out."

"Don't you worry about using names on your radios?" I asked Jess.

"I'm set on an encrypted line. They would have to use our key to unscramble it; otherwise it sounds like garbage or static. They can DF us but—"

"DF?" I interrupted.

"Directional Finding. When we transmit, we make the needle jump. They know somebody's transmitting, but can't listen in. They could hunt us that way, that's why we limit our transmissions and always move shortly afterward. Like we're about to have to do."

"What do you mean?" I asked her.

"My mother and the rest of our happy band of patriots here split the forces at the house. Jimmy was keeping an eye on the Crater crew. He radioed that Jimmy had just returned and said half of the forces were gone."

"They're moving out early?" I asked her.

"Apparently."

I couldn't even trust murderers and crooks to keep their word. Wait... Still, I fumed for a moment, chewing on that. Then I remembered we'd convinced the families to leave and were neutralized by the fact that the Hillbilly Mafia would be rolling into an empty farm. None of the crops were ripe enough to pick, there was no food, and everyone was gone. I once again hoped they didn't torch the place.

"We heading back to the house now?" I asked her, concerned.

"Yes, then Carter, Jimmy, and I are going over to the Crater to wait and watch."

"If you're going, I'm going," I told her softly, reaching over Raider and flattening down the back of her hair that was sticking out of her boonie hat.

"Who is going to watch your grandparents?" she asked me softly.

I mentally cursed. I knew Grandpa and Grandma could handle themselves pretty good when I was younger, and both were full of piss and vinegar... But

85

neither of them would be ready for something like this and shooting the twelve-gauge had bruised Grandpa horribly the last time he'd had to use it. He said that's why he got the lighter one he hung over the door, but I knew that wasn't the real reason. He was getting older, a little bit weaker, and for a long while, he'd been sick.

"Me, but I wish like hell you would stick around too," I told her.

She leaned over Raider and kissed me on the cheek as I fumed. I turned to her, but she rolled on her back, holding one hand up in the universal 'wait' gesture with the other hand to her ear.

"This is Jess, I got it," she said into the mic, then hooked a finger in my direction.

I leaned in close, and she pulled me half on top of the dog and her, kissing me. Raider objected and squirmed out by backing to our feet, making a disgusted sound. I laughed, breaking the kiss.

"What did they say?" I asked.

"That the crew was headed into downtown and away from here. We can head back to your grandparents' place now."

8

CARTER HAD BEEN WAITING with Jimmy when we'd slunk onto the property line from the back, behind the barn where we normally stashed the old tractor. Raider had run ahead of us to the house, unable to contain his excitement, letting out a few playful barks, scattering the few chickens still not in the coop. We'd gone inside and told everyone what we'd seen and how things had gone. Jimmy then cleared his throat and told us his side of things.

"By the time I got there, most of the gang had left, but there were a few pickup trucks heading out. I was able to see ten guys or more per truck."

"How many trucks?" I asked.

"A few. Our numbers have to be off. If I watched thirty to forty men leave, how many were already out there? I mean, they're all armed and some as good as we are," he said, nodding to an AR-15 he'd leaned up against the counter next to him.

"Prisoners?" Jess asked.

Jimmy shrugged. "Hard to tell. They left the women behind. There are some kids there, but for the most part, the people I saw were there by choice. There were a few who had ankle and wrist restraints like you'd use at a courthouse somewhere, but I didn't see many of them. Ten? Twelve? Who knows."

I cursed softly.

"Don't you talk like that under this roof," Grandma said suddenly.

"I... I'm sorry," I apologized. "I'd love to know where everyone is coming from. If you guys had already guessed the numbers at seventy-five to eighty people, and they left the ladies and kids behind... you see what I mean?"

"Before the last truck left, I saw a guy dragging a bound woman into one of the bunkhouse campers. She screamed for a good five minutes while he was in there. I could hear it all the way across the Crater. Then he jumped into the bed of the truck."

"Do you think he—"

"Don't," Grandpa said, and then pulled out a familiar looking flask and handed it to me.

I unscrewed the cap and took a long slug, before handing it to Jess. She shook her head, and I offered it to others who also refused. Grandpa took it gratefully and had himself a shot before putting the cap back in place. The liquor warmed me going down, and seemed to steady my nerves. I wanted to do something. I had no doubt what had been done to the bound woman. She had been dragged into the camper, probably hurt if not raped. The torture of the Guthries had been mild compared to the stories that had come out since their rescue. I just wished we had been able to do more.

Jess' team had focused in on them and were able to split them away with a diversion. An explosion, if I remembered correctly. Then I got an idea.

"Brother, you shouldn't play poker," Carter said, smacking me on the shoulder. "I don't know what you just thought of, but the look on your face makes me think somebody tried to piss in your Cheerios and you're gonna smack them around a bit."

"Something like that," I said with a grin. "Grandpa, do you have any of that aluminum powder left?"

"Sure, but... say, you're wanting to make thermite again?"

"You can make thermite?" Jess asked, perking up.

"He's a chemistry nut. When we couldn't fix an internal part on the tractor he yanked it out. Filled in the void with metal and used the thermite to weld it, before grinding it smooth all over again," Grandpa said.

"My grandson loves his chemistry, kind of like what's between the two of you," Grandma said, totally

89

taking me out of my thoughts. I saw Jess turn a little red in the face as I realized what she'd said.

My mind was racing. What if... what if there was a way to set up some preplanned diversions or traps? Funnel the gang into an area and drop the hammer on them.

"See, he's lost again," Carter said, laughing.

"You know what Tannerite is made of?" I asked them suddenly.

"Um... no, I flunked IED school," Carter said, holding up his hands. "Still got all my fingers though."

The joke fell flat, and I ignored him. "I can take some of Grandpa's fertilizer, some of the aluminum powder left over from the welding projects, and make something similar to Ammonal," I told them.

"Why not just make ANFO?" Jess asked.

"Too big for what I have in mind," I told her.

"What do you mean?"

"ANFO takes at least a stick of dynamite to let off. I can think of a ton of ways to do that remotely, but what if we can sneak something in close enough to make noise. Startle them, get them to come looking?"

"And then you go in and rescue the hostages?" Jimmy asked.

"Hell no," Grandma said immediately, tapping the table with the flat of her hand. "He leads them to look in the spot he wants, and he rains hell down on them!"

"Language," I told Grandma.

She stuck her tongue out and me, then flipped me off. Jessica sat back, stifling a laugh, then wiped at her eyes.

"No, I see how this could work. You can't do anything small with ANFO to a scale like you're talking."

"No, but what if we set up..." I got up suddenly and walked to the TV.

There was a notepad and a stub of a pencil, much worn and chewed. I flipped to an empty page, past Grandpa's old ledger. He didn't use it to track sales anymore, and it was in a code only he knew how to read. I tore out a blank page and came back to the table.

"You remember opposite of where the propane tank was set off?" I asked.

"Yeah, the hill slopes down into the trees. We like to sit there to watch them, because they don't come that way and we have a clear field of fire."

"Yeah, I imagine having high ground would usually be a big advantage," Jess said. "But it silhouettes people coming across that field. It's not been plowed or mowed, and things are starting to grow back, but there's no cover there."

"Right, but what if we lured them into the trees near the top of the hill, then dropped the hammer? Shoot those who aren't killed in the blast?"

"How do you know they might not send some of

the kids or hostages to do that? We already blew stuff up there before."

I hadn't thought of that. "Dammit, you're right."

"Language," Grandma said, a grin on her face at getting me back.

"Right now would be the perfect time to hit them while they're gone," I fumed.

"We don't know when they're coming back, and if they headed into town and not to the farm, are they going there next? Here? We don't have enough intel," Grandpa said, surprising me.

"You were fine with me helping the kids, warning them?" I asked.

"Different situation. They weren't shooting at you."

"Well..."

"What? You forgot to tell me that part!"

Carter held up a hand. "He fired his gun to let us know he had us zeroed in. The farm owner."

"Sumbitch," Grandpa muttered darkly.

"He recognized me, I think. Knows who you are."

"He don't know me that well," Grandpa shot back.

Grandma grinned, watching the back and forth.

"Raider, tell Grandpa to get out the good stuff," I commanded.

Raider had been sleeping on the floor next to me. He rolled on his side and opened an eye, then closed it again. Immediately he started snoring. He was woken by the sudden laughter.

"Your dog has the right idea," Grandma said. "You've been running on fumes, and when it's time to rest you haven't rested," she said and shared a grin with Jessica.

"Now let's not get all into that again," Grandpa said.

"Get into what?" Jimmy asked innocently.

"Ma found the kids rolled up on a hay bale this morning," Grandpa said, cackling.

"Good for you," Carter said, smacking her on the arm. "I told you he seemed like a... er..."

I got up. I was tired, bone weary if I was being honest with myself. I wasn't upset with the teasing, but I felt like we were all talking and playing grab-ass while people were held against their will and hurt. By helping them, I might lead Lance's people our way. How many times could we chip away at them before they figured out the direction we were coming from?

"Everything all right?" Grandma asked, seeing the sudden tension in my expression.

"I... I feel like we need to be doing something," I said.

Raider cracked an eyelid, then let his tail wag a couple times, thumping on the wooden floor before he came to a rest again, without snoring this time.

"Well, we've got to go check things out. Linda's going to have somebody come take our places in the morning," Carter said, pushing himself back from the table and standing.

Jimmy and Jess did the same.

"I'm coming with you," I told her.

"You're staying here, I'll be back in the morning."

"You need to sleep!"

"I will, in the morning, when this is over. We need to get eyes on them again. Hopefully with a fresh set of eyes or two, we can figure out who's there willingly and who's not."

I grumbled, but I knew she was right. I watched them leave, heading once again into the darkness. I paced and finally headed over to the couch and laid down. Raider got up and walked over, sitting in front of it, putting his big head on my chest.

"You got that look again," Grandpa said.

"Thinking about the traps. Might not be a horrible idea to make some and get them ready anyway," I mused.

"No, I think that's a damned good idea, but what is this Tannerite or Ammonal you were talking about?"

"It goes boom?" Grandma said helpfully.

"Yeah, and it can be a small one, or a really big one. You can actually buy it over the counter at the hardware store."

"Oh, that's the flash bang stuff they use on targets?" Grandpa asked.

"Yeah, but we have the ingredients here to make more than just a small flash and a bang. You have bags and bags of ammonium nitrate in the first stall of the barn."

"Yeah?"

"I can make lots of stuff with that," I told him. "And I think we have pounds worth of aluminum leftover."

"And what do you think you're going to do?" Grandma asked.

"Set up tripwire claymores," I told her.

Raider climbed up onto the couch with me. He didn't do this much anymore, as he was nearly fully grown, but he laid across my side until he was tucked between my chest and the couch, his big head on my shoulder. Dog breath blew gently in my face, and I pet him softly.

"How you going to do that?" Grandpa asked.

"Take some of your old mason jars, fill them up with a binary explosive. Punch a hole in the lid, run some 5/16 brake line into it. Get some of your .22 mag rounds... I need a trigger and firing pin..."

I was tired, drifting off. My mind was racing, but I wasn't keeping up.

"You mean brake line? Like the car? The flared stuff?"

"Flared, that's how I'm going to do it. A rat trap, some fish line, a jar and—"

I slept hard and woke up when Raider stirred. I was sitting up, feeling my bladder calling to me when I heard a soft knock on the door. I got up and watched as he ran to it, whining to go out. Who was knocking? What time was it? The house was absolutely dark, early morning light coming in under the crack in the doorway. I walked over and peered out from the side. Jess was there, a smile on her face.

"Come in," I said softly, opening the door.

"Thanks," she said, sitting at the table and unlacing her boots.

"Making yourself comfortable?" I asked her, teasing.

"I could go back to our place, but I'd rather wait and see if they hit the farm today. I want to be closer, in case..."

"I hear you," I told her. "I was kidding anyway, you're welcome any time."

I took her boots when they were off and set them by the door. Raider had shot out the door when she'd come in and I let him back in, closing the door softly again. He went right to her boots, sticking his schnoz deep in one, then the other, knocking them around.

"He's smelling my babies," Jess said, her voice soft and tired.

"And learning more about who you are. Any news?"

She pulled out a small notebook from a pocket and

waved it. "Got notes. Between Jimmy, Carter, and I, we were able to figure out where the hostages are being held, and we know that not everyone is there against their will. Some just don't have anywhere else to go and have decided to throw in with the new regime. They're afraid of the new man."

She'd been out there all night. She must be dead on her feet.

"Who is he?" I asked her. "Not Lance, but the new boss?"

"He's some sort of Negan type—"

"Wait, who's that?" I interrupted.

"You don't know who Negan is?" she asked. "It's from The Walking... you know what, that doesn't matter. It's a biker guy named Spider."

She walked over to the couch and Raider saw her there and ran over, jumping onto the couch next to her, putting his head in her lap. She pet him slowly, lazily.

"Traitor," I told him.

"He's trying to make you jealous, because you locked him up the other night," she said, grinning.

"Oh... well... yeah," I stammered a bit. "How did you know what people were saying, did you get—"

"Jimmy can read lips. Most everyone was sleeping, but there were a few men and women who stayed behind. A couple had an animated conversation at the fire. He only got half of it because one of the guys had his back to him, but that's how. You can do a lot with half a conversation."

"Any sign of Marshall?" I asked.

"No, and no mention either. Oh yeah," she said, tapping her head, "I remember who he is now."

"You want something to eat? I have to go get eggs," I asked her.

"I'll love you forever if you can scare me up some eggs," she said sleepily, one hand half covering her mouth to stifle a yawn.

"Whoa, whoa, moving way too fast for me," I joked.

Raider made a noise deep in his chest. I almost thought he laughed?

"Dork. I'm just going to rest for a minute. I stacked my gear just outside the door."

I'd seen she had her pistol on her hip, but as I moved to the door, I saw her carbine was leaned against her pack. The magazine was out of it. I picked it up and pulled the charging handle. It was clear. I turned back.

"Raider, you want to come outside?" I asked him.

He buried his head into Jess tighter as she worked her fingers through the fur between his ears. This time the sound he made was pure contentment. I waved to them and grabbed Grandma's egg basket and headed out. Foghorn eyed me with bleary eyes, then I remembered being told he was blind in one side. I walked a wide circle around him while he did the same to me.

He half flew, half hopped, and half flopped onto the split rail fence we used to separate the backyard and started telling the world that the sun was coming up.

While he crowed, I walked to the coop and let myself in. The girls immediately perked up and started clucking and chuckling in chicken talk. *Look, kind sir, I made you food! You want to eat our babies? Please, please come take our babies as long as you give us some of the great corn!* At least that's what I imagined their dialogue to be like. I hadn't remembered the corn, but they moved out and into the yard as I collected eggs, already pecking and picking at the ground, grass, and anything with legs they could catch and eat. They were great for keeping down fleas, beetles, and ticks in the area. They would also eat small snakes, worms, flies, whatever. They were nature's almost perfect recyclers. That got me thinking of pigs and how they were essentially the same thing.

There were always reports of ferals, but they weren't a big problem in Murfreesboro like I heard about in Texas. There was an odd sighting occasionally, but I hadn't heard of one in a long time. Maybe I could find some breeding sows that had weanlings?

With the eggs collected, I headed back inside. I was about to show Jess the collection when I saw her slumped to the side. Raider was laying on his back, paws in the air. She'd fallen asleep while giving him a belly scratch.

"Jess?" I said softly, putting the basket on the table.

She didn't stir, but Raider got up and came to me, sniffing at my legs.

"Don't get under my feet," I told him and gently lifted Jess off the couch.

I cradled her close to me. A sleepy smile covered her face and she put an arm around my neck, putting her head on my shoulder. I carried her into my bedroom and laid her out gently. It was hot, so I kept my bed stripped in the summer of everything but a fitted sheet, but a flat sheet would cover me on the nights I needed something. This I pulled over her. She murmured something unintelligible and rolled over on her side. I noticed she still had her radio and earwig in. The red light showed. I turned it off and gently pulled the ear piece out. Then I unclipped her radio and considered the PTT and ear piece but left it.

"You want to stay in here?" I asked Raider.

His tail thumped. Was that a yes? No?

"You hungry?"

He chuffed softly, then ran for the kitchen. I grinned and headed out. Not before I stopped in the doorway though. Jess had stashed her boonie hat somewhere, and her hair fell across her face, obscuring her. She snored softly, almost the sound a kitten made when its belly was full, and it was content, feeling safe. I grinned again and walked to the kitchen. I could hear Grandpa say something from their room, but it was muffled. I put one of Grandma's pots on the wood stove, then poked the ashes a bit and got an ember. I added some small kindling and got it going again before adding a bigger piece.

I'd learned a trick a bit back, though I wasn't sure if it actually helped or not. I'd put a small piece of stove pipe in the flames under the burner. The small fire was still fed air from the bottom, but the impromptu six-inch piece of pipe hopefully concentrated the heat enough to boil that water faster. I had a lot I wanted to do today and didn't want to cook, so I cheated. I rinsed a dozen eggs from the carafe we kept by the sink and then dropped them in the pot of water to boil. Then I added a dash of salt and white vinegar and headed to the pantry. I pulled a bag of dog food out and spilled some into Raider's dish. He looked at me with longing eyes, and I sighed. I went back to the basket and broke two eggs over his food.

He wagged his tail vigorously and began to eat. He never bothered getting them himself, but in an attempt to get him to fatten up, Grandma had shown me the trick. It had worked, and his coat was beautiful as a result of the healthy eating. Still, I had stuff to do and supplies to get. I didn't like to sit around idle while the bad guys were out there, doing things. They had an agenda and a plan. Everything I had been doing lately was reactionary. It was time to be defensive and perhaps offensive in my actions and deeds. That stopped me, and I had to consider, was I the same man I'd been six weeks ago? A year? Did it matter? I'd killed, and I could finally say it sucked to had to have done that... but I wouldn't have changed one thing if I'd had to do it all over again.

I pumped water, a chore I usually put off until later on, but I hadn't done it yesterday at all. The carafe in the house was all the fresh water we had left at the moment. I filled three buckets and carried them in to find that Grandma was up. She had her hair pinned back, but she was dressed, or as dressed as retired people who didn't get company usually were. She had on some sweat shorts and an old Razorbacks t-shirt.

"Good morning, Grandma," I said softly.

"Morning, Wes, I see you got some eggs already," she noted as I carried two of the three buckets in. "Want me to fry you up an egg?"

"I've got a dozen or so in the pot of water."

Grandma made a face, we'd had a lot of boiled eggs over the years.

"Get me some mustard seed, and some oil out of the pantry... oh and some dill."

"Okay," I said, walking over to it.

I flipped the switch and stood there a second, wondering if the lightbulb had burned out. I'd done this a lot, and realized even out here in the sticks, that I'd grown up used to having power more often than not. I opened the door wide and stepped back to let in as much light as possible. I found what I needed right away and set everything on the counter for Grandma.

"Do you have any of your old canning jars you're not particularly fond of?" I asked her.

"Why? You thinking about doing something like you were talking about last night?"

"Yeah, I was thinking that case of them with the chipped tops..."

"You go ahead, Westley Flagg, you know I was leaving them for you and your grandpa. Should have about two cases out in the barn near the junk pile."

"Yes, ma'am. Thank you," I said, grinning. "One more thing, where's the mouse or rat traps?"

Grandma let out a half-exasperated sound, then went into a drawer we hardly ever used. She pulled out a brown paper bag that had been flattened down to fit. I opened it up and saw a dozen traps or more.

"Haven't had any rat problems around here since Grandpa let the furry bastards have it," she said with a grin. "Try to bring them back if you can."

"If things work the way I know they will, they'll probably go up in flames if not blown apart, Grandma."

"We can find more, I'm sure, or make more. You and your grandpa were resourceful. I just wish your mother..." her words trailed off, and she looked away.

I walked up behind her and wrapped her in both

my arms, hugging her tight. "What do you think happened to Mom?" I asked.

"I haven't heard from her in a couple years now. Moved to someplace in Seattle with her new husband I guess?"

I hadn't heard any of this.

"She got remarried?" I asked.

"We would write letters from time to time. I usually would get one with her current phone number, and I'd call up. She moved around so much and had so many different numbers over the years..."

"Why didn't you tell me?" I asked her.

"She asked me not to. Of all the things she did wrong in her life, staying away was the best thing she ever did for you."

I hugged her tighter, then let her go. Raider was still eating noisily, but he had slowed, his tail wagging.

"You're probably right," I told her. "I love you, Grandma; you did good by me."

"I just wish my daughter would have grown up the way you did," she said, her emotions coming through her voice.

"A lawbreaker who loved chemistry and booze?" I asked.

She turned, pushing me back. "Only reason you broke the law was to help us, and you weren't hurting anybody. Your mom... She does, but not directly. Little things, mean words, never... Please, can we talk about this some other time?"

I nodded and backed up for the doorway. Something on my belt hit and I looked down at the radio. "Grandma, if I leave this in here, can you get me or wake up Jess once they start talking on it?" I asked, turning the speaker up and putting it on the counter by the sink.

"You got it. I'll run you some food out when I'm done. Going to the barn to work?" she asked.

"Yes," I said, grabbing the bag of traps up again.

She gave me nod, so I headed out. Raider followed.

TANNERITE IS A BINARY EXPLOSIVE. THE INGREDIENTS are simple, but Ammonal was the generic name with a slightly different set of chemicals involved. It would all go boom if mixed properly. The thing about Tannerite and the generics like it is that it took being hit by an object going about 2,000 feet per second to set it off properly. I'd learned all about this stuff in college, where some of the guys in class were into pyrotechnics, making fireworks and planning to do stage show stuff. Still, in chemistry, a lot of work goes into having stuff NOT blow up when you don't want it to. I could flip that around and make some defensive or offensive things.

The first thing I did in the barn was find the two cases of jars. They were right where I'd thought they'd be, in a bin near a couple of washers and dryers stacked on their sides, close to where I'd caught Marshall poking around in here. I dragged them into the shine room and hit the button for the LED lights. They came on, driving the shadows away. Next, I went and unlocked the stall where Grandpa kept his chemicals stored, along with an old wooden box. I wasn't completely lying that Grandpa had a powder room. He had dynamite all right, what the old timers called powder, but he didn't have very much. A few sticks. It would have to get buried sooner or later; it was old, and the nitroglycerine was settling out.

I wasn't there for that though; I was there for the fertilizer that was stored as far away from everything as it could be, in a tin box Grandpa had made himself and riveted. He'd claimed he'd done it to keep the moisture of the floor from getting into the fertilizer, but I knew he was worried about other things splashing on it or coming in contact with it. See, there were some things chemically that were just plain nasty. Ammonium Nitrate and aluminum powder were two ingredients used to make a lot of things that went boom, flash, or would start a fire. They were also pretty mundane chemicals.

Now that I was thinking the opposite of how I'd learned things, I could think of dozens of ways to use my college education to take common everyday items and—

"You want a hand with this?" Grandpa's voice startled me.

"Sure," I said, turning.

He walked over and set down a box of lids and rings on the pile of jars I'd stacked on his chair.

"What are you going to do?" he asked.

"I'm going to fill a jar three quarters full of fertilizer and use about two tablespoons of aluminum powder. Going to have a hole through the lid with some 5/16 steel tubing, then drop a .22 caliber shell in it. I was working out the rat trap idea, and I think I've got it figured out," I told him.

"Rat trap? Wait, what are you going to use for a firing pin? If it was a rim fire, I think I know what you're going to do."

"That's what I was thinking, and it'll only have to work once... but what about a bead of solder on the bottom of the bar, right over a hole we drilled in the trap, that the makeshift gun goes into?"

"Why do you need to shoot a bullet to blow things up?" Grandpa asked.

"You need an impact from something going about 2,000 feet per second to make it light up," I told him. "Here, grab your hand drill and I'll go find some brake line or fuel line. I know I have some around here somewhere—"

"It's over in the far corner near the spot you wanted to put pigs."

Right. I nodded and hurried off.

It was an ugly duct taped monstrosity when I was done, but it was done. Grandpa had used the unflared side of the tubing to mark a hole where the trap's bar would come down, and carefully drilled it out. It didn't have to be perfect, but it only had to work once. I said that over and over, but there was no rushing him. I'd filled a mason jar the way I'd described to him, then pushed the tubing halfway inside it, leaving about six inches sticking up over the lip of the jar. I punched a hole in a lid, and put that down there, sealing the mess up with duct tape. The flared end of the tubing sat in what ended up being a cut out notch on the end of the rat trap. I spent most of my time trying to make a bead of solder in the right spot and was able to get it done when I got the hang of the heat again. To make sure the trap didn't wobble, I'd duct taped that too, to the tubing, leaving the primer free.

To set it off, I'd set the trap, run a trip line or pull line to the bar trigger. It'd snap shut and then...

"One problem," Grandpa said.

"What's that?" I asked him.

"Cut the tape off the lid and pull the damned tube out," his voice was harsh.

"Why?" I asked him confused.

"This bomb of yours has a hair trigger and it's about the most harebrained but dangerous thing I can think of."

"What?"

"How many times do you accidentally set off a mouse or rat trap when you're trying to put it down?" he asked.

I always did... and then I saw what he was getting at. Just because I could make it into a simple and cheap bomb, it was as much a risk to me setting it, as it was to anybody else who tripped it. Also, without adding anything to it, the glass would work as the shrapnel, but if I really wanted to be nefarious about it I could add in rocks, nuts, bolts, ball bearings... My imagination spun ideas around my brain.

"You're right," I conceded. "I'd never make a good mad bomber; this would have blown me to hell and back."

"If that stuff explodes the way you say it does, how about making a safer and easier way to set off the bullet?"

"What do you have in mind?" I asked him.

"Get me the map gas torch; I'm going prospecting in the trash bin. You got more of that steel tubing?" he asked, already moving off.

"I do..." I answered, hesitantly.

"Good, you're going to need it!"

"Westley," Grandma's voice called from outside. "Breakfast."

"You coming?" I asked him, brushing my hands off on my pants.

"No, you go inside, clean up, and have a good sit. I already snagged a couple of your boiled eggs," he said with a grin. "I'm a tinkerer like you, or at least I was. I got me an idea or two on how to do this. Oh, and make sure you leave the solder. I'm going to need it."

"Ok, Grandpa."

"Oh, and get me some more of that tubing before you take off. I'm going to need a lot of it."

"For what?" I asked him.

Grandpa just laughed, rubbing his hands together. It was unsettling and, when it became apparent he wasn't going to answer, I went inside.

9

GRANDMA TOOK one look at my hands and how sweaty I was and refused to give me food until I cleaned up. I headed into the bathroom and made sure I had my towel and stripped. I was going to have a quick cleanup today. I didn't heat water for a bath yet. We'd suspended a bucket from the ceiling of the bathroom by a lightweight chain from three hooks, terminating into one that hung from the handle. The bucket had an outlet on the bottom as this was one of our former smaller scale brew buckets. Push the button for the outlet, air temperature water sprayed out. Get yourself wet, lather up, then rinse yourself off.

I did that and then considered things as I sat looking in the mirror. I needed a shave. The door pushed open, and Raider stepped in, his tail wagging. I opened it up more, and he walked inside.

"What are you doing, buddy?" I asked as he inspected the bathroom then spun around and walked out.

"I think he was showing me where you were," Jessica said, rubbing her eyes.

"I'm sorry, did he wake you up?" I asked.

"No, your grandma did. Said breakfast was almost ready."

I could smell it. Her sourdough was already legendary in my mind, but it smelled like she was toasting it. What was she making?

"Said I needed to get cleaned up, but I didn't know it was occupied. I just followed—"

"The little traitor," I said with a grin, making sure my towel was tight. "I was going to shave real quick but you can have the bathroom if you need it."

"Thanks."

She looked absolutely tired, her hair mussed, her eyes dark from going a day and a half without rest, but she was still one of the most beautiful women I'd ever seen.

"Can you bring my pack back to me?" she asked, starting to strip.

I didn't want to be a perv and watch, but I paused for about half a second longer, before she made a rude gesture at me. Grinning, I walked out of the bathroom, Raider at heel. I got her pack and saw Grandma roll her eyes as she noticed me in a towel.

"The furry mutt let her in," I explained, "I'm just going to drop this off for her."

"Uh huh. If you two wait too long to come eat, I'm going to feed your sandwiches to the dog here."

She wasn't making an idle threat. I hurried to the bathroom, holding the towel in one hand, the pack in the other. I knocked twice, then cracked the door and shoved it through.

"That my pack?" I heard Jessica ask as the water hit her behind the shower curtain.

"Yeah, setting it by the toilet. Your towel from last time is hanging up."

"Thank you, and if Grandma feeds my sandwich to the dog, I'm going to be upset," she said, though I could tell she was smiling by her tone.

"Then hurry up," I told her and closed the door quickly.

I dressed even faster than I imagined I could. The view of myself in the mirror showed that I had gotten leaner than I remembered myself. It hadn't happened overnight, but over the course of weeks. The far-ranging effects of the power going out had trimmed off the small bit of fat I'd had on my frame. No more was I taking my truck everywhere, that was too loud. I was walking or using my bike to keep noise pollution to a minimum. My clothing had started fitting a little loose, but that was what belts were for. I ran a quick comb through my hair, then headed to the table.

Grandma had just put the percolator on the pot holder. The coffee was still perking, the boiling water spurting up into the bulb on top. The holder kept the kettle from melting Grandma's plastic table cover. I grinned at the sight. She'd made two squared off loaves of sourdough at some point yesterday and had sliced and toasted half a loaf of it. She'd made half a dozen egg salad sandwiches, steaming hot.

"You going to wait for Jessica to eat?" Grandma asked.

"That would be polite, wouldn't it?" I asked her.

Grandma rolled her eyes, and I had to fight back a grin. She'd set the table for four, though I wasn't sure that Grandpa was going to be joining us. I'd heard no explosions or gunshots from outside, and my furry threat detection machine was wagging his tail furiously, so I knew nothing was amiss. I sat down and poured myself a cup of steaming coffee before stacking my plate with two sandwiches that had been cut diagonally. Grandmas never change.

"You going to leave some for her?" she asked.

"Half, I left her half?" I pointed out, wondering why that wasn't enough though, there were actually four left.

"Boys," she said to herself and turned to the sink.

I rolled my own eyes and took a big bite. It was ambrosia. Raider whined piteously, though I knew he'd already eaten. Knowing I was risking dog farts, I grabbed a slice of bread, then squeezed and wiped some of my egg salad on a piece and held it down for him. Three bites later, it was gone. He started licking my hand in appreciation. Grandma was staring at me when I looked up, so I wiped my hand on my shirt and popped the piece of sandwich I'd started on into my mouth. She was about to say something when Jessica walked in.

She had put on a fresh pair of jeans and a tank top, but she had my white button-up on again, the one she'd only worn for an hour or so yesterday. It was open in the front, but the back was damp from her hair, which had been braided quickly. She saw the food, her eyes going wide. She looked at me, and I motioned for her to sit next to me. She pulled out a chair and then looked at my plate. I handed her a sandwich half from my plate and started in on another one.

She took a bite and made an exaggerated sound, her eyes looking straight up.

"How did you make this mayo?" she asked, through a mouthful of food.

I was going to answer, but I also didn't want to risk a smack to the back of my head while my mouth was full. Death by choking on egg salad was big on my list of nopes today.

"Raw egg, cup of oil. Mix in some salt, seasoning of choice and whip it up," Grandma said, matter of factly.

I kept eating and handed Jessica another sandwich half off my plate. Raider pushed his way between us and was making a whining sound, putting his snout on Jessica's side.

"Grandma, this is amazing," she said, stealing my coffee cup and taking a sip.

I grabbed another cup to the right of me and re-poured myself a cup, so I could have my own.

"Thank you," she said. "Sometimes the old ways are the best ways."

"I don't know if making food like this is the old ways, but it's better than anything I've ever had or made myself," I told her seriously.

Hunger does funny things to people. It makes bland food taste fantastic; it makes lightly flavored water taste like nectar. I'd been hungry, almost starving, at a couple points in my life. I knew for a fact that both Grandma and Grandpa had gone without meals a time or more to make sure I had enough. This wasn't hunger talking, this was Grandma's mastery in all of its glory. She made country cooking on a woodstove an art form.

"Has the radio gone off?" I asked, grabbing another sandwich half from the pile in the middle of the table.

Jessica's eyes got big, and she slapped at her side unconsciously.

"Nope. Just making these funny little ticking noises."

"Can I see it?" Jessica asked.

Grandma brought it over to her and she put it on the table, food forgotten for now. Grandma sat down across from me and grabbed two sandwich halves and poured herself a cup of coffee as Jess played with buttons, twisted a knob, and then punched in some numbers on the front.

"This is J," she said, "Any word?"

"All is silent," a feminine voice came back over the radio. "Far eyes found a group in town, going through the grocery store and trying to get into the bank. Had a party, now sleeping it off in the middle of a ring of trucks."

Her mom?

"Good to know. J out."

"Bear out."

"Momma bear?" I asked her.

Jess turned a little red in the face and nodded. "You wouldn't have been able to hear anything on this handset without the code. The signal's encrypted. In the old days, that was illegal, probably still is, but none of that matters now."

"Well, no news is good news, right?"

Raider went stiff between us and started growling. All three of us went rigid and I started to get up, Grandma as well. I motioned for her to sit and walked to the door. When I'd gotten dressed, I'd put my pistol on my hip out of habit. I reached for it slowly. I heard a click behind me and saw Jess had followed, and had pulled the charging handle of her AR. I nodded and turned back to the window. A male figure slunk out of the tall weeds, approaching the barn, and slipping inside.

"You know who that was?" Jessica asked, her breath hot on my neck.

"No, and Grandpa's out there tinkering with stuff," I said, suddenly going cold.

"Will your dog stay silent?" Jessica asked.

"Sometimes. Raider, no barking, be quiet; Grandpa depends on this."

Raider chuffed from about three feet behind me. I didn't know why I trusted that he understood me, but in the heat of the moment, he always seemed to. I opened the door slowly and, when I didn't see anyone coming from the woods or tall grass, I slipped out.

"You stay in here," Jess said behind me.

Whether or not she was talking to Raider or Grandma, I wasn't sure. I heard the shotgun's pump action being half worked, checking to see if it was loaded, and surmised it must have been Grandma. I walked quickly, zigzagging like a deer would, toward the barn. Noticing him making it to the barn door took maybe ten, fifteen seconds. Nerves and adrenaline would do funny things to a person's perception of time, and I noticed that my vision was starting to dim around the edges. I knew what this was and knew people from the military knew how to avoid this. I would have to ask Jessica about this someday as it would be helpful in more than poaching when buck fever kicked in.

"Cover right, I got left," Jessica said from my back left. "Raider, wait for Wes."

Gun in my right hand, I grabbed the swing door in my left, my right bracing it, and pulled it open roughly on its oiled rollers. Two figures stood up straight, startled at the sudden sound. My pistol went up covering everything from twelve o'clock to three o'clock. Jess was next to me, her carbine sweeping twelve to nine. I recognized Grandpa right away, and my aim turned to another figure who was putting his hands in the air as a furry bullet ran between Jessica and me. An inarticulate scream came from the figure as Raider latched onto his leg without slowing, and took the man down, turning him with the momentum.

I holstered the pistol as I moved, not wanting to call off the dog yet. I hadn't seen a weapon, so over whatever it was Jess was yelling, I literally jumped onto the figure, straddling their side as they protected their delicate bits from the bite of the furious Shepherd. Raider broke off as I pulled the man's hands away and then froze.

"Marshall?" I asked.

"Hᴏᴛ ᴅᴀᴍɴ, ᴛʜᴀᴛ ᴀʙᴏᴜᴛ ꜱᴄᴀʀᴇᴅ ᴛʜᴇ ᴇᴠᴇʀ-ʟᴏᴠɪɴɢ ꜱʜɪᴛ out of me," Grandpa said, wiping his hands on his overalls.

"Language," Jessica chided.

Grandpa stuck his tongue out at her, and her laugh was almost musical, "Just kidding. I've said and heard worse. A lot worse. You can't offend me."

"What do you want to do about this guy?" Grandpa asked, hitching a thumb in Marshall's direction.

"The other side wants him bad. He smells like shit and looks like he's been through the wringer. Let's take him inside and clean him up some, get him some food. I bet he'll be more than willing to talk."

A very hogtied and gagged Marshall nodded his head enthusiastically.

"I don't know, maybe we should get what we want outta him, then feed him to the hogs; they've been a hungry lately."

He shook his head at Grandpa's words comically, but I could tell he didn't know that he was being put on.

"He's going to be good, he has to; otherwise Raider's going to sic him in the balls," I said stone-faced, remembering the movie *Stand By Me*.

"Ouch," Jessica said theatrically, cupping imaginary plumbing.

Marshall made some sort of sound, so I pulled the

gag off and the rag out of his mouth. He sputtered and spit a few times.

"You're the last family I would try something with," he said seriously.

I could tell he meant it. He hadn't wet himself, but his eyes were full of unshed tears. He was terrified and running on empty.

"Good, let me get you untied, but if you try anything, Raider will run you down. I know in your condition, you can't outrun him, let alone a bullet."

"Yes, sir, I'm sorry I'm here," he said quickly and then went silent as I started on his legs.

GRANDMA WAS ALMOST LATHERING MARSHALL WITH attention. Raider looked a bit jealous and ashamed at the same time. His story had started coming out in spurts as soon as Grandma had offered him the rest of the sandwiches and fresh coffee. He'd devoured it entirely, and before he could finish his stories, she sent him to the shower to cleanup. I'd been in some rough fights, but he looked like he'd been at the wrong end of several somebodies.

"Boy that dirty, I wouldn't normally let him sit at the table," she said to me, "but he looks half-starved and beat. Those bruises on his arms and neck weren't from you guys today."

I hadn't noticed the bruises on his arms because of the caked-on sweat and dust.

"Go get him a change of your clothing..." I raised my hands up in protest, but she waved a hand at me. "Now don't you sass me. I'll get his cleaned. If half of what he said was true, he might have come to the only place around here that can help."

"I... yes, Grandma," I said and gave up.

"Do you have any more of that egg salad?" Jessica whispered as I was leaving the table.

"I'll show you how to make some later on," Grandma teased, "but I can make you a sandwich out of some sourdough and cheese?"

I had almost eaten my fill, but that made my stomach rumble. We'd traded a while back for some cheese with another vender when Grandma had last been at the farmer's market, and we hadn't gotten into it much. We had a few smaller rolls of it that had been dipped or coated in wax to keep it good for storage in the root cellar. Raider ran ahead of me and jumped on my bed, sniffing the sheets then burying his head.

"That's where Jessica was sleeping," I told him, turning to my dresser.

He gave out a low woof and then jumped off, running for the front of the house. I shrugged and pulled out a pair of jeans and an old plain white t-shirt. I had plenty of those, and I gave him one of the less stained ones. I wasn't going to ask for the clothes back.

"Wes?" I heard from the doorway. He was still sort of dripping water, a towel draped around him. "Somebody took my clothes?"

"Probably Grandma," I said, and laid the jeans and shirt on the edge of the dresser. "Dry off and put these on. Sorry, not giving up my underwear. Those get precious in the apocalypse." I was half serious, but half joking, and I got a smile and a nod in response.

I pulled the door closed behind me and went back to the table. One of the cheese wheels had been taken out of the restocked pantry, and several thick slices were on a plate next to the sourdough. A pint jar of leftover mayo and a knife were next to it. I quickly made up a few sandwiches with both Grandma and Jess watching me. I was suddenly ravenous again.

"Where's Grandpa and Raider?" I asked suddenly.

"Your Grandpa got a couple cheese sandwiches and headed back to the barn. He said he was almost done. Said you and Jess could handle Marshall if he had mischief in mind."

"Shenanigans," Jess said, smiling between a mouthful of food.

I put a sandwich on her plate and then offered one to Grandma. She smiled and took it.

"Wes, I really can't thank you enough," Marshall said, coming back into the room, stopping when he saw the plate of food.

"Dig in, you look starved," I told him.

Jess pulled out a chair and I sat down next to her, across from him. My pistol dug into my side, reminding me it was there. In a way it was comforting, though not from Marshall, but rather the knowledge of what had happened at the crater of diamonds.

"*Spider and his guys showed up almost as soon as we got settled. They brought a lot of people and trucks and campers with them. He was somebody Lance knew from the big city. I think they used to... uh... be in business together.*"

Marshall's words were easily recalled.

"*I think it was meth. I think Lance was cooking it and giving it to Spider to sell. That's how he got enough money to buy the Barred Rooster. Why he didn't ask our family for a loan is beyond me. I don't think he wanted my dad to find out. Anyway, when Spider showed up with ten guys, we thought cool. Nobody else is going to attack us at the camp there and shoot people.*"

Was he really thinking of our rescue operation of the Gutheries as an attack? They shot themselves, not us.

"*Then more guys showed up, and after the third group of his showed up, most of the later ones on Harleys, they came for me. I was trussed up and thrown into the bed of a truck and driven out into the country somewhere. They held me in an old shed. I saw Spider once after that; he told me that they were holding onto me while they negotiated with Lance. I only saw his guys after that. They told*" *me if I tried to escape, they would track me down and kill me.*

"I heard their plans though. They camped outside the shed and waited for word from the big guy himself. They're going to kill Lance after they take total control of the area, and they were using me as leverage to keep him from going to war against them."

There had been a ton more, lots of little details that had Jessica needled him with, but she had held off on a lot, because today was the day they were going to hit the farm and she wanted her mother and a few of the crew from their bunch to 'interrogate' him.

"We need to warn my cousin," Marshall said with a mouthful of food.

Grandma took her sandwich and poured herself a glass of water from the carafe and walked out. Raider followed her, but didn't leave; instead, he returned and sat next to me. I turned to Jess who was turning red, but not from embarrassment.

"Your camp wasn't attacked by anybody we know. We rescued the bakers from your cousin and set off a distraction," Jess said.

"Rescued? Lance said that they had come to him, but they got into a fight?"

"Where the hell were you then?" I asked him.

"Most of the time?" he said around a mouthful, "I was trying to find enough food. The first people that were shipped out of Murfreesboro didn't get everything taken from them like the guard did soon after. I was finding places with food for the guys with the trucks to unload. Sometimes I'd find entire stretches of houses—"

"To steal from?" I asked him. "What if people were counting on that food when they came back from wherever they were taken?"

He quit chewing and put his head down. I could see his ears turning red, probably from shame. Jess looked at me, her eyebrows raised. I shrugged.

"There's no food. We even checked the trains that stalled along the tracks. There were a few we couldn't get the locks off of, but the ones we could were full of useless stuff. Dead electronics, car parts, sometimes cars. Nothing we could really use except for the gasoline. We found plenty of that."

Jess sat bolt upright and shot me a look. I shrugged as Marshall looked up.

"I don't know what to do. A lot of us would have starved if I hadn't gone looking for food. I'm not proud of what I was doing, breaking into people's places, but when you're hungry..."

"You do things you'd never imagine yourself doing," I said, remembering Emily and her own admission about how their husbands had died trying to become... raiders? Murderers? Marauders?

"I know me, and Jesus will settle up someday,"

Marshall said, "but I did what I had to do. I pray for forgiveness every night."

"How did Spider's men grab you?" Jessica asked.

"I was in town, the neighborhood near the grocery store," he said, wiping his mouth, "I was looking for food when a truck full of guys pulls up. I recognized them all and figured they were there to load up supplies to take back to camp. Spider was with them. I should have figured something was up from that." He went back to eating.

"I have to call this in to my mom—"

"*A woman and child just broke cover from the edge of the woods...*" a voice crackled from the radio.

"Do you know who?" another voice asked.

"*Looks like one of the mothers from yesterday. The small lady,*" the voice crackled at the end, but I could make out her description, "*and a kid, maybe five or six?*"

"Emily and Mary," I said quietly.

Jess put her hand across mine. We listened as they gave the report. The two had broken cover in the field furthest from the barn. The kid—Mary? —had been on a dead run, being chased by the older and more lithe Emily. The reports were cold and dry as the events were being described. The girl got into the barn half a step ahead of her mother and both were lost out of sight.

"*Can faintly hear her calling for Mary,*" the voice said over the radio.

"Stupid, why are they back?" I fumed.

"*I can hear motors firing up,*" the voice over the speaker said and in the background noise and crackling of the radio, I could too.

They sounded like chainsaw motors, but I knew what they were. Smaller two stroke motors or quads. Similar to what I'd heard when the three men had been chasing Les.

"They need to hide," Jess said.

"*A dozen dirt bikes and quads just broke cover. They were under some sort of ground cloth that blended in. They are converging on the barn. Wait one. The woman and child are running for the trees.*"

"Shoot them," I snarled at the voice on the radio.

"There's only two men watching the farm right now," Jess said, "They can't take on a dozen or more men."

"They can do something—slow them down, let the girls get away," I said, snatching for the radio.

"*Shots fired, not from us,*" the voice on the radio said. "*Two men to a quad or dirt bike and two sets of people just went over. Another shot. Coming from the woods?*"

"That crazy bastard," I said, suddenly feeling a glimmer of hope.

"The grandpa?" Jess asked, and I nodded to her. "Have them open fire."

"*Trucks entering the property. Took us by surprise. Couldn't hear them from the commotion and shooting.*"

Dammit. Raider whined, probably sensing my sudden tension, and I dropped hand to my side as he licked it, comforting me.

"Must be forty men here now. Woman and child were tackled just now. Shots keep coming out of the trees, but the men are returning fire. No more men down, some that went over are getting up."

We listened in horror as the report came in, and an explosion over the radio surprised us all, making Marshall twitch and jump in his seat.

"Firing from the tree line has stopped."

"Was that a grenade?" Jess asked into the handset.

"Pretty sure that was two or three grenades," the reply came, and for once the voice sounded upset.

We listened as the voice told about the woman and child being trussed up and thrown unceremoniously into the back of the pickup truck. The group went through the barn and the house, a few into the tree line. Within an hour, they were gone, leaving the buildings intact. Marshall had gone from pale to bone white during everything. He'd stopped eating and his hands had a shake to them as if he had some sort of palsy. Jess turned off the radio when it was apparent there was nothing more to report.

I'd eaten more than usual today. The mantra *sleep is food and food is sleep* had been drilled into me by Grandpa as a kid growing up. Both of them fed the body, but right now I was feeling a lump in my gut and it was making me nauseous.

"Marshall, this is only part of what your cousin Lance has been allowing to go on lately," I told him, trying not to snarl.

Enough of it got out that Raider looked at me in surprise, then back to Marshall, his muzzle pulling tight, showing teeth. He started growling low in his chest, and the rumble of his anger could be felt through the seat of the table. Jess put down her hand and he didn't look up at her as she stroked his head.

"I didn't know, I swear," he said.

"Yesterday, they dragged a woman into a trailer and raped her, for the entire camp to hear."

"I swear, they had me locked away for a week, week and a half?" He was almost pleading, but the tears from earlier were back and they were falling freely now.

"This is partially your fault," I raged. "You're going to tell Jessica's people everything, and I do mean everything." I stood up.

"Where are you going?" Jess asked me suddenly.

"I'm going to blow off some steam," I told her. "You can come or watch the kid or bring him with—"

"Calm down, you're not thinking clearly," Jess said.

Raider stopped growling and looked up at us.

"I think I am. I am not going to be helpless anymore," I said softer.

"Let me get Marshall to our people or have them come here."

"I'm just... I'm headed to the barn. I need to get my mind off this a bit."

Jessica nodded and when I stalked to the door, Raider followed. Grandma waved from her seat on the front porch.

I FILLED ten jars the same way I'd filled the first. Instead of putting a hole through the cap, I put them on tightly. I heard movement behind me, figuring Jess or Grandpa had come to see what I was doing. Honestly, I'd thought Grandpa would still be out here working. I had almost wanted to be left alone, but he often could see things clearer than I could. Even when my heart knew what to do and my head was conflicted, my grandparents were always the ones I turned to for the tie-breaking votes when it came to moral decisions.

The barn was empty, but I saw that he'd moved stuff away from his workbench. The solder and torch were over there, along with assorted nuts and bolts and some lengths of tubing. I ended up using his other end of it for pouring the chemicals. I had the rough sketch of a plan working in my head. The more I thought, the more I was ashamed that I had not acted sooner when I strongly suspected what was going on over there. I blamed myself for a time about the man I killed. Maybe I had focused on that so much to cover my own shame and feelings of guilt because I *KNEW* what was happening at the Crater.

Jessica's people were watching that group, so they had to have known as well. For how long? I almost dropped what I was doing when a gunshot rang out behind the house, but I carefully put the last jar on the bench and pulled my pistol and raced to the door. I saw Jessica coming out of the house, her carbine in her hands.

"Was that you?" she called as we both ran for the middle of the yard where the well was.

"No, it was behind the barn somewhere. My grandpa in there?"

Another shot rang out as we got near each other, and I heard no telltale sign of a bullet whizzing by, but that didn't stop us from zig zagging as we used the scant cover we had between the barn and the back side of it. I was tempted to run through the barn, but the back roll away door wasn't used or oiled like the front. It would make a lot of noise and until I knew what was going on—

Crack! Another shot rang out.

We flinched, that one was close, but we couldn't tell what direction they were shooting. Jessica made a hand motion to me. I tried to puzzle out what she was saying as a furball went racing past me, barking happily.

"Raider!" I shouted and barreled forward, forgetting cover.

"Wes, wait," Jess called, but both Raider and I came to a halt.

Grandpa was sitting behind the barn, a grin on his face. He bent over something and fiddled with it as Raider walked up. He ruffled his hair and then stood up.

"Go see your dad," Grandpa said gruffly.

Raider looked at him hesitantly then to me.

"Grandpa, what are you doing?" I asked him, seeing three empty shell casings on the stump he was using as a bench, the brass gleaming.

"Your grandma told me what happened. She had the window open in the kitchen. She's nosey like that. With those hooligans taking the ladies and kids and leaving, I figured it was time for me to test out my invention."

"What if they're coming this direction to cut through the woods like we do? Did?"

"Never have before. Come take a look!"

"Raider, sit. Stay," I commanded.

He did, so Jessica and I walked up slowly. She saw what he'd done and let out a feminine giggle, somewhat out of character for her. Then I saw it. He'd taken an eyebolt and had put bends in the end with the eyelet. He'd brazed the straight shank to a piece of one-inch flat stock and drilled and bolted another eye loop at the other end. That one was ground down, probably painstakingly by one of Grandpa's files. Through that was what looked like a roofing nail. It was long and had something wrapped around the diameter of it near the head between that and the eyelet. I bent closer and saw that it was a spring, and a triangular notch was filed into the nail as well.

The triangular notch fit perfectly in the filed down portion of the eyelet. A piece of fish line was tied to the head of the nail. Then I saw what was in Grandpa's hand. He was using his thumbnail to pry out a shell casing from some steel tubing.

"Couldn't figure out what length to use, so I tried out a few sizes. It just slides in the far eyelet."

It was simple, safe, and beautiful. It was literally a better mousetrap. The nail was the trigger and the firing pin. When pulled off the notch, the spring sent the nail forward, the tip hitting the primer. That would send a shot down field, which was a much, much safer version of what I was trying to do.

"That's brilliant," I told him after a minute, suddenly feeling self-conscious at my word usage.

"I don't figure that you learned nothing fancy like that in that there college, did you?" Grandpa asked.

Raider barked, and I smiled, shaking my head no. A commotion with the chickens behind me had all of us turn to see Grandma stalking forward, Grandpa's pump shotgun in her hands. When she saw us all standing there, she put the barrel skyward.

"Bud, what in the Sam Hell do you think you're doing, you asshole?!"

"Language," Jessica and I chorused.

Grandma gave me a dour look, then used her first two fingers to point at her eyes then at us. She was watching. She turned and started walking back to the house, the shotgun held loosely in both hands now.

"YOU REALLY DON'T HAVE TO TIE ME UP," MARSHALL said for the hundredth time.

"Shut up," Jessica said. "It's for your own safety anyway."

"Why?"

"If they see you untied and walking next to me, they're going to think it's a trap and turn your stupid melon into pink mist from a distance. You're Lance's cousin, and my family never was too fond of Lance to begin with."

"Because you two used to be a thing?" Marshall asked.

I wanted to butt stroke him with my rifle, but I didn't. I'd gotten my kit out and was cleaning guns, waiting for it to get dark. Jessica thought she had talked me out of doing anything, but as soon as she was gone, I was going to start my plan. I hadn't told Grandpa, but he knew somehow. I'd seen Grandma take my pack to the counter, and throughout the day she'd sneak something into it. Half a roll of sourdough bread. My face netting. Small bottles of water. Hard chocolate she'd stashed somewhere that Grandpa and I hadn't known about.

I was going to war. I knew it was stupid to say that, when I had real warriors and a real soldier in the area, but they were unwilling. The odds at the camp were overwhelming, according to the repeated conversations I'd listened to on Jessica's radio. That's when I pretended to throw in the towel. Jessica, low on sleep, napped for a while and Grandpa sat with Marshall. Actually, if he was going to escape, he had his chance when we'd all run out back in response to the gunfire, including Grandma. Instead, he remained sitting at the kitchen table, his hands folded neatly in front of him.

"That's one mark against Lance," Jessica said. "The other is kidnapping people, torturing them, killing and raping and so many other reasons."

"Please don't hurt my cousin. He's the only one

who ever looked out for me." Marshall's sincerity had me do a double take.

"Where did you go to school?" I asked him suddenly.

"I didn't, well... I did, but I was home schooled." Marshall's sadness dried up, as he looked at me with a curiosity.

"Why is that?" I asked him.

"My parents thought I was too sensitive to go to the regular school. Said kids might pick on me."

Guys who were like your cousin.

I didn't say it aloud, but I thought it real hard. Still, Lance had been his protector. Was he autistic? Emotionally delayed? The first time I'd met him I'd known there was something slightly different about him and, despite everything he'd been through, there was still something slightly different about him. Where he should be a raging monster of insanity, or cowed, broken, he was neither. It was same shit, different day.

"Emotionally impaired?" Jessica asked him.

"I don't like that label," he answered immediately.

I shrugged. He'd never shown any strange behaviors, except for a weird way he handled his emotions and an almost Darwinian level of curiosity that had led to me almost shooting him before. To make things more confusing, Raider, who'd been sleeping on the couch, perked up and walked over. He sniffed around everyone as Jessica was tying his hands in front of him and licked Marshall's elbow. Marshall flinched but then saw the teeth weren't out. Still, he didn't relax.

"Raider is telling you that he's going to trust you not to hurt Jessica and not to get her hurt," I told him.

"How can you know that? He didn't say anything?" His confusion was evident from his expression.

Raider sat down and barked once, sharply.

"He said he knows things, so quit being a butthead."

Raider chuffed, and Jessica grinned at me. "You're finally learning his language?"

"I think so," I said as she finished binding his hands in front of him, an eight-foot tether coming off the end that she could hold.

"Learn that in the service?" I asked her.

"No, I was practicing my knots to show you some-day," she said quietly, shooting me a wicked grin.

"It's been thirty-five years since Grandma last tied me to the bedpost," Grandpa said suddenly from the La-Z-Boy.

Jessica must have forgotten they were in there, and she turned a deep crimson red. Of all the times for him to hear something clearly...

"That's because I wanted to go fishing!" Grandma shot back from his side.

"Fishing did happen!" he retorted, loudly, "Took my pole out and everything!"

I covered my ears for a moment, shaking my head

at the sudden bickering and disgusting things my grandparents had started saying. Jessica fell into the kitchen chair, her hands over her face, her ears so red I thought she was going to have a heart attack.

"Why would you tie somebody up to go fishing? Ma'am, we're not going fishing, are we? I thought we were going to talk to your people?" Marshall asked innocently.

"Dead, I'm dead," Jessica said, laughter coming out as she was face down on the table now, her forehead banging against it softly, her whole body rocking with barely restrained laughter.

"She looks pretty lively to me," I told him, "and Raider and I are trusting you to listen to her and to keep her safe," I instructed Marshall, suddenly serious again.

The bickering stopped, and Jessica's funny bone must have dried up. She sat up, wiping her eyes. She started to say something, but then stopped, nodding at me. She understood why I said that to him. Now that I sort of had Marshall figured out, I could understand him and understood why a monster like Lance, as bad as he was, thought this one man needed protecting. He had all his mental faculties, but he was innocent and was probably as emotionally mature as an early teenager at the very most. He hadn't been exposed to much of the evil in the world. That was why he barely registered the abuse he'd suffered himself.

Marshall gave me a solemn nod.

"I still don't understand what this has to do with fishing," he said, looking at his bound wrists.

This time, it was Grandma who lost it first. Then we all did.

I WATCHED them leave at dusk, sticking to the northern edge of the road on the slope. It would be harder going for Marshall, but supposedly they had some sort of transport arranged, or a meeting spot. Jessica wasn't clear on that, and I hadn't pushed. It was like she wasn't clear on their family compound out on the logging land, even though we were basically together now. Maybe not after tonight though. I prayed she'd forgive me for what I was about to do.

"They ready?" I asked Grandpa, who was carrying a burlap sack with a squared shape in the bottom.

"Yeah, paint's barely dry. You're going to smell like Rustoleum as you go out there," Grandpa said softly.

"As long as I can see the yellow stripe, I can shoot them in the dark."

"Grandson... again, what you're doing is..."

"Stupid, irresponsible, going with my gut when my brain says it's a bad idea?"

"All of those things," he said, handing me the sack, "and exactly what I would have done. I'm proud of you. In case... Well, let's not say, but I want you to know that I'm proud of you. You've done as much for your Grandma and I... I..."

"I love you too, Grandpa," I said, trying not to choke up. "Keep my dog for me. In case."

"In case?" Grandma said, carrying my pack to me. "In case of what?"

"In case I don't come back. If something happens, let Jessica's people know, and get to them. I think she'll make sure you're taken care of."

"You can't take the whole camp on yourself," Grandma said. "Jessica's people won't do it either. Their group isn't big enough and they've got military help, remember?"

"I won't try to do that," I told her, "I'm just going to do my own watching and waiting. If I see a chance to right a wrong..."

"That's what I was hoping you were going to say," Grandma said. "I was kind of hoping for grandbabies someday. That's why I was glad to catch you rolling in the hay with—"

"Grandma," I said softly and pulled her to me, hugging her tightly.

She surprised me by hugging me so fiercely she

143

almost squeezed the breath out of me. She held it for a heartbeat longer, then pushed me back. In the moonlight, I could see her eyes watering. I wiped a tear off her cheek and hugged her again.

"This isn't goodbye. I'm literally going across the street and into the woods and across another field to watch. I'm sure Jessica's people will be staked out there as well. Jimmy even."

"And how are you going to make sure they don't think you're one of the bad guys when things get hot?" Grandpa asked.

I pulled the radio off my belt, the one Jessica had given me, and handed it to him in trade for the sack of wrapped IEDs.

"If they call, tell them I'm doing what I do best," I told them.

"Keeping your head down and your nose clean?" Grandpa asked.

"Hell no, that I don't listen to others very well," I said, cracking a grin.

They both nodded, but Raider chose that moment to jump up, putting his paws on my chest. He'd grown a lot since I'd first found him, which I saw now as we were practically eye to eye. He licked my chin and then rubbed the side of his face against my chin. I pushed him back gently, then patted his head.

"Losing moonlight," I said as the moment turned melancholy. "Raider, you stay here."

He sneezed at me, which suspiciously sounded like he was swearing at me. Grandma gave a low whistle and he cocked his head to the side, looking over to her.

"With me, Raider," she said, patting her leg.

He sat down next to me. "Ok, Raider, you stay here with them. If you cause them any problems, they're going to take away your morning eggs."

Again, he sneezed. I rolled my eyes and gave everyone a nod then started walking. I figured Raider's disobedience and mouthing back at me meant he wasn't going to listen, but I was surprised to see, when I looked over my shoulder, that the three of them were standing in the same spot. I was going to have to repack my backpack to get the sack of Ammonal bombs out of my hands soon, but I didn't want to do it right there at the homestead. I didn't want that to be their last memory of me.

I WAS SCOPING OUT THE SPOT I'D MENTIONED EARLIER TO Jess and Grandpa and decided that if she had any doubts about my sincerity of leaving this alone, she'd place somebody there. So, I picked the next best spot I could. It was risky, as I'd found out the first time, but going back there would be the least likely area that Jess, Linda, or her father would suspect.

Despite what Grandpa had thought, the paint on

the jars was dry. He'd run a stripe across the lids, leaving the rings on. I could pop a canning lid at any distance I could see in normal circumstances, but this was a large field and the trees didn't give a direct view from all angles, plus it was dark. That was why I decided to set my diversion near their vehicles. I had thought about it, and I rather doubted that the Hillbilly Mafia would allow the prisoners free access to the vehicles. It just didn't make sense. Plus, if I could catch a few of the bad guys in the blast while taking out their vehicles...

I was thirsty. I pulled my pack off and slid out one of the two canteens my grandma had snuck in behind Jess' back. I uncapped one and started to chug when I felt the warm burn and the sweet flavor of Grandma's doctored up lemonade. I swallowed about half, then spit the rest out and changed canteens. Liquid courage would be welcome tonight, but I couldn't get sloppy. Still, I'd made it in and to the far southwest corner of the field and would traverse north until I got to where they were parking the trucks and bikes, away from the RVs and camper trailers.

The moon wasn't as bright as it had been on other nights, but there was enough of it for me to make my way easily through the gloom. I'd spent many a night like this, checking Grandpa's traps or stalking deer, hoping to get them silhouetted so I could get a shot. I'd even taken the old poaching gun, the .25/270. I'd made sure the suppressor was fitted properly after my drink and decided to sit for a bit and see what I could spot through the binoculars I'd packed.

Anybody could see the bonfire from a distance. It was easily ten feet across, and the flames seemed to rival the height of the trees around the field. After a summertime of no plowing or upkeep, the grass was easily thigh high now, so I had to kneel to do it. I could make out figures around the fire. Some were holding sticks near the flames, maybe cooking food. Others stood further back, arms folded. Some were dancing around, and I could hear snatches of laughter and what sounded like excited cheering. I kept panning, and tried to focus in on the darkened campers, wondering which one the ladies were being held in. It was likely where Emily and Mary were being held.

A figure moved into my view and was gone. I panned again, almost missing it when a thin man walked to the fire. He held his arms up, and people seemed to settle and close ranks around him. I couldn't hear what he was saying, but when I tried to zoom in on his face, I lost the focus. By the time I got it back, the crowd was packed too tight around him, with the fire blocking the rest of the group. Time to move.

I shouldered my pack and got the rifle off my shoulder. It was loaded, with every pocket in my pants, shirt, and overalls weighed down with the plastic cartridge holders Grandpa had donated to the cause. It was way more ammunition than I'd need. With a bolt gun, I doubted that there would be any call for almost sixty rounds of hand-loaded ammunition, but that was how much I'd brought. If I had more, I would have brought it all, but that was all we had.

Besides, I could always throw rocks at them if I ran out. I patted my pistol through the side opening to make sure it was still in place under my coveralls and then got going again. I was moving slow, but not at a crawl. Nighttime was my friend, and I was trusting years of instinct and experience... and praying that none of Lance's guys had night vision capabilities and sentries out; neither of which I had seen evidence of.

"Not long now," I said softly to myself.

Grandpa had given me six jars of Ammonal and three of the triggers he'd made up so far—though I wasn't planning on using them—and three pints of thermite he'd mixed up special. I knew how horribly dangerous just powdered aluminum was alone, but we'd added in the special sauce, and if things went well, the diversion Jessica's group had constructed before was going to look like cheap fireworks in comparison to what I had in mind. I just wished I had more fuse. Another forty feet would have made me happy.

I WAS MOST OF THE WAY TO THE TRUCKS WHEN THE HAIRS on the back of my neck stood up. I flattened myself to the soft mat of tall grass and took a deep breath. Nothing had really triggered an alarm response directly, just a gut instinct. I couldn't smell anything except for the campfire and my own sweat. I didn't see or hear anything to concern me. That didn't stop me from pulling the rifle off my back, and I worked it in front of me slowly in a prone position. I strained, but I couldn't hear anything nearby. That was when I realized what it was that had made my adrenaline dump in great buckets full.

There were no night sounds. I was far enough away that I should have heard more than just the raucous party at the fire, but I didn't. I didn't know what time it was, but I knew it had to be long after midnight by now. Hours and hours and hours after the raid at the farm.

"...Danny, you queer this deal for me and I'll bury your ass in this field," a voice said suddenly.

"Hey, man, it's not my fault—"

His words were interrupted by what sounded like flesh on flesh impact. He'd just gotten decked or kicked. I heard a body hit the ground and then retching. They sounded like they were right on top of me, but I could see a good ten feet in every direction. Sound was funny out here at night sometimes. They were probably twenty or thirty feet away. And Danny, the name sounded... it was the pedo. My jaw clenched, and I held the gun a little tighter.

"I swear, I wasn't even looking at her," he protested.

"Even James is tired of your shit," another voice said, and I heard a heavy slap and a surprised intake of breath. "You damage the merchandise, and I'll personally cut your heart out and feed it to you."

"You got no problem taking the ladies for a turn, you hypocrite," his words came out in a sob.

"They ain't kids, and the women were given a choice. Keep. Your. Hands. Off. The. Girl." Each word was punctuated by a slap. "She's going to be worth a fortune, whereas your value to us keeps shrinking by the day."

"You know," Danny's voice got a little louder, "you put your hands on me again, and I'll make sure you're hung out to dry."

The threat hung in the air for a moment

"Yeah? With what?" The voice sounded hesitant.

"I'll let Spider know you're the one who forgot to lock the shed. That Marshall bastard is still—"

I heard another thud and then a commotion. I risked getting up on a knee and saw that the two figures were rolling around on the grass, kicking and cursing at each other from no more than twenty steps ahead of me. I heard shouts further back, somebody calling out for Danny and Steve. It was too dark for me to make out the features of the men, but I was high enough that I could see that one was straddling the other, raining heavy blows down on him. I was about to flatten myself down and start creeping out of there when I saw a flash of moonlight reflected off something in the man's hand. It plunged down, and an agonized growl or groan escaped the other man's lips. I started backing up slowly, keeping the rifle between me and the men.

The man on the ground started making a high keening noise, and I could hear the impacts of flesh and then the soft begging. I could hear Danny, as he was stabbed close to fifteen or twenty times. It had shaken Steve's confidence, Danny's conviction that he could get Spider to believe him about how Marshall had got loose. Apparently, it was enough of a threat that it was worth killing him over. I saw the figure stand up, the one that must have been Steve, and then bend back over. He stood up a second later and tucked something into his belt. He had sheathed his knife after wiping it off on the dead man's man shirt.

"Danny, Steve, where are you?" a voice called out of the darkness from a distance.

"I'm headed back," Steve shouted, "don't shoot."

"Where the hell is Danny?" another voice called back.

I could hear the sound of feet moving through the tall grass at a fast clip. They were making a lot of noise. They were coming in loud and fast, and I didn't want to be overrun. I got down on all fours and moved out as quickly as I could until I was against the edge of the tree line again. Once I was there, I was able to stand up within the darkness and peer out. I could see the large group of men, and they were shouting and shoving at one in the middle who had his hands up. I heard him repeatedly mention the little girl, but through the binoculars I couldn't make out features of the men in front of me.

There were at least seven or eight men there, and I did the best I could with the binoculars to memorize every face. The moon was helping, but there were still shadows from the trees on the edge of the field that were blocking a couple of them from my sight. I got a good look at Steve and, although by Danny's allegations, he was a rapist, and bad shit had been going down here, he had kept little Mary safe, for one more night at least. I wanted more information about what he was talking about, how they were going to be worth a fortune. A fortune to whom?

I started moving away through the shadows, dodging tree branches and moving slowly and softly. I felt my way to the north end of the field, my feet probing for dry, brittle sticks that I might not see beneath the old leaf litter that was under the trees. When possible, I stayed out of the field. Keeping an eye on the group of men became difficult, but I could hear them moving off in the direction of the campfire.

Three men were pushing and shoving another one, and I had to figure it was Steve, but I wasn't sure.

I stopped when they got close to the bonfire then got the binoculars back out. I leaned against a tree to take some of the weight off my back, and scanned what was going on, praying I wasn't reflecting light back at them. A tall, thin man stepped out of the crowd, the one I'd seen earlier with his arms raised. He was wearing dark clothing, and if I had to guess it would be leather or jean material. Black, maybe? I was too far away to tell for sure, but I could see his exposed skin and face easily in the firelight. He put his hands up and made a motion as if to quiet the group of men, and then started speaking.

He spoke with Steve, who motioned back in the direction they had been in. And then he made some kind of gesture, pointing at one of the nearby camping trailers. It was the bunkhouse, judging by the description I'd heard from Jessica's guys. I was glad to know, or at least have a good idea, where the prisoners were being held now.

I was close enough to the trucks now and pulled my pack off.

Grandpa had wrapped a spare shirt in between each of the jars. The smaller jars with the fuses were what I wanted right now, and I got those out first. A quick scan and a listen had me hopeful that there was no one hanging out at the vehicles at the moment. The last time I'd snuck over on this end, a fight had broken out between two different sets of people, and several had been shot. I didn't want a repeat of that, especially as I would potentially be one of the people shot.

My goal tonight was to disable vehicles and hopefully create enough of a distraction to get close enough to the trailer to make stuff happen. It wasn't a fancy plan by any means, but considering everything that was going on, I doubted they were ready to be hit in the same fashion they'd been a week ago. Who would be stupid enough to do that?

The first two pickup trucks I came to had their tailgates down, the back of the beds full of old debris and junk. Still, a pickup truck is a pickup truck. It doesn't matter the make or the model, the gas tank is roughly in the same location.

I would have loved to have known how much fuel was left in each tank. In an ideal world, I would target trucks with tanks that were only a quarter full, because that would give room for fumes to build and expand within the gas tank, and that would go perfectly with what I was about to do. I worked my way slowly to the front, near where the motorcycles were parked. The truck with the topper that the couple had been rolling around in last time I'd been here was gone, something that stuck in my mind but probably meant nothing.

I picked out three likely looking trucks and set the jar of thermite right over the bed. Each of the pint jars had about three feet of fuse, which was nowhere near enough for what I wanted to do. I would have to get each of them lit and run to the next truck. My best guess, with the old adage of twenty-five seconds per foot, I had seventy-five seconds or one minute and fifteen seconds after I lit the first fuse to place two other charges and light those as well. I was going to have to move fast, and hopefully not draw attention to myself.

The next part was going to be a bit tricky. I had half a dozen Ammonal charges. I had seen videos where just a pound of it was enough to launch a push mower in the air and had been used to demolish things. The trick tonight wasn't to kill people, despite how I'd felt earlier. Tonight's trick was to disable their vehicles. Without the vehicles, they would be forced to march everywhere. That is, if they didn't just find more that were working. Most of what was here represented the economy used car lot, but it was the mid-south, and everybody had an old Chevy or Ford that never quite ran right.

PLACING the Ammonal charges was a little more difficult. I wanted them near the bikes. Why in the books I read did the bad guys always have bikes? In real life, they had mostly American trucks, but there was a dozen Harleys and a couple Goldwings here, representing something different. Comfort, maybe? I found the Sportster I'd just recently seen. I had to wonder if that was who'd knifed Danny just a little while ago. Steve? Was he Bandana?

The yelling and commotion from that area had died down long ago, and I'd used that distraction to do my work as quickly as I could. I was going to light off the thermite, hoping to catch a tank with a bunch of fumes in it. In the movies, things blew up in a dramatic fashion. I was hoping for much the same. During the confusion, and with them trying to put out the fires in the trucks, I'd shoot two of the jars with the yellow stripe. I placed one of them under the Sportster that Bandana had been riding. I had to hope that Danny's was the other one, now forever without its owner.

I grinned at that. If things hadn't been so urgent, it would have made more sense to just let them keep killing each other.

I was about to light the first fuse when a noise caught my attention. I backed into the trees and looked over to see several men arguing, a good ten or fifteen feet away from the main group at the fire. Unlike the tall, thin man from earlier, who seemed to hold everyone's attention, one of the figures here wasn't just tall and thin, he was almost gaunt. The guy looked like a walking bean pole, but I could make his features out in the darkness and the dancing shadows from the firelight.

I made sure my backpack was on the ground, and pulled my rifle up, looking through the scope. It took a while to get the sight picture, but I was able to make out his face a little bit better. The guy wasn't gaunt from lack of food, but built lankier than I was, and he was scarred up in a way that suggested he'd been burned or had a really bad case of road rash at one point or another. Pink keloid scar tissue covered part of his face and neck, with thick, dark hair growing longer and wild. The moonlight and dancing rays of the fire were giving me a lot more illumination than I had expected. He was tall and powerful.

Spittle flew from his mouth as he screamed insults, pointing a big finger in the face of the man who'd stabbed Danny. I shifted the scope a bit and saw dark spots covering the man's face and neck as he moved around, keeping room between him and the big man. Danny's blood?

"...was going after the little girl!" I finally made words out, desperate and angry sounding words.

Both were moving this direction but were nowhere close enough to make me out. I was adept at moving in the darkness and being quiet. I had to be to keep the family fed, and to help Grandpa with the moonshining. Now I was using those skills to hopefully save as many people as I could. I'd never set out to be a criminal but considered myself something of a modern-day outlaw. I would follow the law if I could, but circumstances... I cut that thought off as the big man backhanded the other. The slap was so forceful it sent the man who'd stabbed Danny crashing to the ground. He got back to his feet slowly.

Was this Spider? I had him in my crosshairs. If this was him here, I could take care of a lot of—

An angry wasp buzzed by me and a second later another one punched my left shoulder, rocking me back. If I hadn't had my sling wrapped around my left hand, I would have dropped the gun because my right hand immediately slapped at my shoulder, coming away slick. Something hit the tree right behind me, sending splinters exploding, tearing into the back of my head. Then I heard the echo of the shots as I realized I hadn't been stung after all. I fell to the ground, hiding behind the truck as two more shots rang out. I crawled part way under the truck for cover.

The pain hit, and it was bad. My whole body suddenly convulsed as the spot in my shoulder seemed to be connected to every nerve ending and screamed for attention. I heard shouts and a radio crackle nearby. I couldn't make out the words, but the big man was yelling orders, drowning out everything else except the gunfire, and that kept pouring in just over my head. It was dark out, I was invisible, I had been quiet; yet somebody was raining gunfire my way.

"Red team, form up. Our guys say they nailed somebody messing around near the trucks. Blue Team, take Lance's boys and go secure the hostages and get a good count, I want to know who's missing, if any. Green Team, watch for another ambush. Cover me and Red Team, and we'll see if the target is down like the snipers say."

The words were emotionless, but given in a loud, commanding voice. A voice that had practice directing and guiding others. And... three color coded teams? I suddenly had an idea of what I was up against, and it terrified me. I was about to become hamburger if I didn't move fast. Luckily, I was partially under one of the trucks I intended to use as a distraction. Except now, the distraction might save my life. Maybe.

My left arm was useless when I tried pushing myself up; instead, I had to roll over and sling my rifle with my right hand and fumble in my chest pocket for the zippo. I found it and flicked it open, lighting it. Warm flame greeted me. With a hand that was shaking more than I'd like to admit, I lit the first fuse and then dragged my backpack with me to the next truck, waiting for a bullet to hit me.

"Where did he go down?" the man who had to be Spider yelled.

"Blue Chevy," a voice crackled over a radio somewhere.

They were close, too damned close. I had seventy-five seconds? Rough estimate? Would that be too long? I made it to the next fuse and lit it about a foot from the end. It lit after a few moments, burning in two directions. I hurried to the third truck, running up right now, the gun banging on my back. Nothing hit me, and I made it to the last truck. I forgot about fuse length and lit it before closing and pocketing the lighter. I dropped the pack, got the rifle off my back, and put the pack on, almost screaming in pain as I worked my left arm through the strap. Precious time was going, and I could smell the fuse burning off next to me. Any moment now the first truck would light. I didn't want to be anywhere near it.

Having got my load adjusted, I slinked into the tree line. Even if the sniper had thermal sights, seeing me would be a chore, and I had trees to use as cover now. Bright light lit the sky behind me, and I hurried. The thin sheet metal that was used as the bed of the truck wouldn't hold for long, the gas tank probably only half a second longer. Shouts behind me let me know I had surprised them at least. Good.

"Put it out—"

A loud thunderclap precluded a pressure wave of warm air. I half turned, seeing flaming debris fly everywhere, and an enormous fire spreading out from where the truck had been. Several figures were wreathed in flames, screaming. I spied all of this from behind trees and bushes as I moved stealthily out of the area, back the way I'd come. Another thermite charge ignited, the light much brighter and harsher than the gas tank explosion. I'd had no idea that this would work this well. At worst it would have disabled the trucks, but at best... I was seeing it right in front of me. It was going as I had hoped and prayed it would.

The second truck exploded, and a heartbeat later something flew past me, tearing a huge hole in the foliage. I hit the dirt and turned to see that the truck had gone up, spewing fire and flame in all directions. What had flown past my head? Was it shrapnel?

Screams punctuated the night, and I couldn't make out the words over the crackling of the flames. Then the night lit up again. There was no WHUMP sound, but the screams were loud. In the secondary fires, I saw figures moving and the tall grass start burning and spreading across what was usually a freshly turned field that people had prospected for diamonds in, before the power had gone out in the world.

With no explosions happening for a moment, I slid down a tree and pulled my pack into my lap with one hand. My side was warm and wet, and I needed something to stop the bleeding. I dug through the pack with bloodied hands until I found a pair of clean socks. I undid one of them and folded it and pressed it against the spot I'd been shot. The pain was worse, and the entire entry wound throbbed. I looked up quickly to make sure I was still safely hidden, and saw human shapes running around. I could hear shouts, screams, and curses, but nobody came my way.

I was sweating heavily, and it was more than the usual heat we had in the late summer. I took the other sock and bit down on one end, using my mouth to hold it in place as I fished the other end out from under my armpit. I dropped the wadded sock I was using as a pad. It took me a few minutes, but I was able to tie the sock around my armpit and shoulder and get the wad in place, so it was holding constant pressure. No exit hole in the back of the shoulder. Well, shit.

Communications were one of the things my preps had lacked, medical supplies were another. If I got out of this, I would have to figure something out. Maybe Carter? Would he help me after this? I looked back out to see that the fire was being fought bucket by bucket. Where were they getting the water? How had they organized so quickly? I put my pack in front of me and pulled my rifle over. Using the pack as a rest and trying not to use my left arm as I looked through the scope.

Dirty, sweaty men and a couple figures I thought were women, had organized a bucket brigade and were busy working on putting out the grass. The trucks had been parked in a spot that had been hacked into the brush, and it looked like those were going to burn also. I grinned. At least something had gone right. I couldn't get an angle on the bikes because of the spot I was at, so I moved to the right. I gasped as a new bolt of pain shot through me, but I managed to reposition myself.

I had just focused my sight picture when I saw a figure hold up something to eye level, then shout. Spider stepped out of the bucket line and shouted a question, but the words were lost in the chaos and madness. The person shouted back and held the object up higher. A mason jar with a yellow stripe. I was shaking from the pain and adrenaline, and I knew I was losing blood, but I wasn't done yet. Not even close.

I focused, clicked my safety off and took a breath. I

163

let it out slowly as I took in the small amount of slack in the gun's trigger. I adjusted my aim up about two inches from the top of the jar to take into account the distance. I couldn't adjust for wind because the fire around the figure was being fed by small gusts from every direction, and I couldn't make a determination. It was a long shot at a small object, but I'd done farther shots before, but never while injured and bleeding.

Three. Time slowed down for me, I blew out my breath as slow as I could.

Two. My heart beat, lub dub.

One. The shot went down range, the gun surprising me as it should, when the trigger was pulled.

I lost the sight picture for a moment, but an explosion rocked the compound for a fourth time. I worked the bolt and found half the bucket line had fallen or were running. I couldn't find the big man or the figure who'd been holding my jar up. Nobody was looking in my direction; the suppressor had done its job well. I focused on the furthest out of the now re-forming line, wondering if they thought something had cooked off. Didn't they know I was after them?

A man with a rifle across his sweat-stained back was the first one I focused on. I vaguely recognized him and realized he was one of Lance's boys. The bandage around his wrist... What was his name again? I fired. He fell as if poleaxed, his bucket dropping. I worked the bolt, swinging the gun to the right again, looking for the other ammonal charge, but the area where the bikes had been was all fire and carnage. I swung the rifle back. Several figures were running away from the man I'd shot, probably realizing that this was no accidental fall. I focused on somebody shouting at them, a pistol in his hand, and started taking in slack from the trigger.

"Right where I thought you'd be," a voice said from behind me.

I looked over my injured shoulder to see a rifle butt half a heartbeat before it hit me in the face. Pain exploded from my temple, and a heavy weight fell on top of me.

13

SORE. Head hurt.

I rolled over and couldn't help puking. Somebody was washing the side of my face. The girl I'd met at the party? How humiliating. That was it, I was never drinking Jim Beam again. I was sticking to Grandpa's shine, where we stripped out more of the bad stuff than commercial distilleries—

I tried to push myself out of my puke, and my left shoulder wouldn't hold my weight. In fact, it screamed in pain. I opened my eyes and winced at the brightness. Daytime. I wasn't at a frat party like I'd first thought, I was lying in a dried puddle of blood and puke. I heaved again, moving my head so I wouldn't spray it across myself. I saw the dead man to my right and smelled smoke. Something large and furry moved into my sight and licked the side of my face, then chuffed.

"Raider?" I croaked.

He sat down, and I could see most of his body before collapsing on my right. Something poked me in the side and I moved, finding my pistol underneath me. Had I drawn it? Fired? I couldn't remember. Little gremlins were running jackhammers behind my eyeballs. I could smell something resembling a trailer or house fire, a forest fire and charred meat. I grabbed my pistol and dropped the magazine one handed. One cartridge missing. I sat up slowly, Raider's tail making a swish, swish sound as he wagged it. His hind end started to wiggle, and I knew a happy bark was coming next, so I was quiet, but firm.

"Shhhhh, I don't know how long I was out. There's probably people still around here."

Raider got down on his belly and looked at me, his head cocked to the side. I was desperately thirsty, so I pulled my pack to me with my good arm. I wanted water, but something told me I might need a little more pain management. I uncapped the container with Grandma's special lemonade and downed half of it in one long swallow. I capped it, feeling the alcohol and lemonade hit my insides. Fire bloomed in my stomach, and my body wanted more. I knew with the blood loss I needed water more, so I sipped at it slowly and looked at my surroundings, trying not to puke. My head felt like a rung bell.

I was roughly in the same spot I had shot from. The floor of the forested area had been trampled flat. The dead man was wearing what looked like night vision goggles, but I wasn't an expert in that. I pulled them off, finding the power button and pressing it. That was how I'd been found and probably how they'd been able to get a shot at me. With those off, the man I was looking at seemed rather clean cut compared to the others I'd been looking at through the scope last night.

He had a tuft of white blond hair, brush cut close, and a trimmed mustache. He was wearing black BDUs which had a scorch mark and a rather large hole in the heart area... and had a matching backpack that had either been dropped or come loose. I was guessing, but after butt stroking me, the man had jumped on me, trying to take me alive. Somewhere in the craziness, I must have pulled my pistol and shot him. I'd woken up to Raider cleaning my face during a dream... Right?

"You're a good boy, come here," I told my dog, wincing as I shifted my weight.

Raider came and sat next to me as I started going through the man's pack. I found two magazines for what I had figured was an AR or M4. One magazine had green tipped ammunition, and the other looked like plain ball ammo. I set those aside and kept digging. The man had his pack set up like I did, with everything he'd need for a day or two in the field. I found two extra sets of batteries and a charger for the NVGs if I had to guess, and put those in my pack, not wanting to take the time to bother with them further. They were electronics, and he carried them. They somehow worked, despite the solar storm that had knocked out everything else. I added those to the pile with the NVGs and magazines and kept digging. Nothing else in the pack caught my interest so I turned to the corpse. He had died almost immediately if I had to guess, because for somebody who had been shot in the chest, there was very little blood. His heart must have stopped right away.

Most of what he had on him were things you'd expect a guy to carry. Knife, keys for something. Wallet. His clothing was of no interest either. Somewhere though, he had a rifle. If nothing else, I wanted to take it with me. It would be one less gun to worry about at my back. I rubbed my face and winced. I felt like I'd been laying out in the sun for a few days. I got my pistol and made sure it was functional before holstering it. I saw my rifle and shuffled that way. I found the dead man's rifle on the ground next to mine. Raider whined quietly, but I made a shushing sound.

I looked over the dead man's gun. The receiver of the gun had a selector switch that made me do a double take. Somebody had made this piece custom, or it wasn't a regular stock receiver. It had three settings. No Pew. Pew. Pew, pew, pew. I grinned and set it on safe. It came with an oversized optic on it. It wasn't a scope I saw but something that looked like a red dot. I turned the knob on top and saw a red, then green dot turn on. I turned it to the off position and pulled first my rifle and then the M4 over my shoulder with the provided slings. I crab walked back to the backpack and pile of loot, careful not to use my left hand.

Raider whined as I wobbled. I sat down hard, dizzy. The blow to the head was the last thing I remembered, but apparently, I'd surprised him and shot him while dazed. Why hadn't anybody come looking for us? A wave of nausea hit, but I breathed heavily and waited until the spell passed. I needed to keep as much of the liquid in me as possible. My throat was dry, and my head hurt, but I could move. If I could move, I could get home. Why hadn't they found me? I hurriedly packed the pile of loot from the dead man into my pack. I repositioned everything, almost screaming in pain as I got the pack's strap over my left shoulder. Then I got both rifles back on and tried to stand.

Raider walked up, licking the side of my face. I was too tired and half dead to push him back. I made a rude sound and he stopped, getting back. I tried to get up again, but everything was too heavy. I went to my knees and right hand, grabbing a sapling. I tried to inch myself up. I was about to give up when Raider got under my chest and pushed. I let out a cry as I used my left arm, but I was able get upright. I looked to my left, north, and gaped.

Over half the field of grass had burned, and there were piles of twisted and charred metal where the trucks and bikes had been. Two or three of the trailers were nothing more than burned out husks on flat wheels. There was nobody in sight, but I could make out buzzards circling above and some on the ground. I almost puked again, but knew I wasn't too far from home. If they had another sniper waiting on me I was dead, so with nothing left to lose, I got moving, lurching tree to tree, to have something to hold onto. I was so tired, I hurt so bad, and I felt so sick. My shoulder was throbbing in time with every step, every heartbeat, but it didn't seem to be leaking.

"Raider, how'd you get out?" I asked him as he shadowed me.

Raider whined and, instead of walking ahead of me, he stayed behind or next to me. I shouldn't have expected an answer, but I could tell he wasn't happy to have found me in the condition I was in. He had probably escaped from Grandpa and Grandpa and come tracking me. A deep bark sounded about thirty feet from me, and the both of us stopped. Raider got in front of me and growled deeply, his hair standing straight up on the ridge of his back.

My heart started racing and my vision dimmed.

The nausea and brain fog seemed to double as the figure of a bear materialized in front of us. Raider started barking loudly, making fast starts and lunges. My mouth was dry again, and I was about to puke when another two figures stepped out in front of me. The world was going dark at the edges, and I was trying to free the M4 I'd taken from the dead man. My legs went loose, and I fell to my knees. Raider turned to look at me and rushed back so he was immediately in front of me. I was retching, despite seeing a humanoid figure and two huge bear looking things.

"*Nein, Pass Auf,*" the figure said in a guttural language that sounded familiar.

My body went limp, and I realized that I was passing out. Raider was sitting now, his tail wagging, making a happy sound. Didn't he know the bear was going to eat us? He should run, he should—

I GROANED. MY ENTIRE BODY HURT, AND EVERY BUMP jolted me. We were traveling through brush, and I was tied down to something. I could see saplings at the edges of my shoulder, with paracord holding my chest, arms, and legs to something I was strapped on. A travois?

"Raider," I said softly.

A quiet woof sounded close by, and I turned to

see my pooch walking beside me. The movement stopped, and I heard another guttural command and the travois seemed to settle down to the ground. I saw movement, then a green canteen was handed to me. I was scared, disoriented, and I was thirsty. I swallowed the liquid gold greedily, noting it was not Grandma's doctored lemonade, but still something sweet. I drank until it felt like an ice spike formed between my eyes, and I winced. Liquid rolled down my neck for a moment, and the canteen was withdrawn.

"Don't worry, Westley, we've got you. Raider found you for us," Jessica said, coming into my vision.

I was hallucinating. Jessica was in front of me, but she was in camo again. Her face was smudged, and it looked like half of her hair was singed. She had what looked like blisters on one hand, but she was smiling. If this was a hallucination, I could at least enjoy it. I smiled back.

"Take me to your leader," I said, my head rolling to look down at my boots.

Two packs were lashed there, mine and another one that matched her camo.

"You're looking at her," Jess said with a grin. "I really thought we'd lost you."

"Grandpa and Grandma?" I asked, coughing.

"They're fine. Worried sick. I radioed them as soon as Diesel and Yager tracked Raider to you. You passed out. Raider was going full on aggro on us until he realized it was me. Good thing he likes me, huh?"

"That makes two of us." I grinned stupidly at her.

I wasn't making sense. Something was wrong, but I hurt too much to know. I was burning up, but the nausea seemed gone for a second. A warmth was running through me. Wasn't dying supposed to feel cold?

"You goof," she said and brushed her hand against my cheek, while using her other hand to wipe something out of her eye.

"How long...?"

"Three days after the explosions."

"I've been out for three days?" I asked her, surprised.

"Listen, I have some guys about to be here to help carry you out. Save your energy, I don't know how you survived those fires, but you're horribly dehydrated, probably concussed and you lost a lot of blood. I'm not a medical, expert, but..."

Her words trailed off, but I was tired again. She slapped my face a couple times gently, making Raider give out a warning growl.

"I'm just waking him up enough to give him more electrolytes," she explained to him as the canteen was put back to my mouth.

I drank greedily. Three days? How had I survived that? Three days without water, and I should have been dead. Had I come to at some point and gotten into my pack and not remembered it? Apparently, I'd killed the man who'd brained me and didn't remember it. My stomach started to cramp a bit just as the canteen was taken back.

"How is that?" Jessica asked.

"Too much, not enough," I said.

"You need surgery and medication. When we're out of here, I'm going to have your grandparents meet us by the road, but then you're coming with me."

"Where?" I asked her.

"Our facility," she said quietly, going still.

Raider's tail had been wagging but stopped, and he went rigid and looked hard at something behind me. Jess turned to look as both Yager and Diesel started growling as well.

"Marco," a voice called.

"Polo loco," Jess said, surprising me.

"You found him," a deep voice said, and heavy footsteps approached us.

"He's in bad shape. We have to get him into surgery; he's been shot and out here for a few days."

"Septic?" The voice was deep, like two boulders rumbling together.

"No, but I think he's got an infection and a concussion," Jess said to somebody behind me.

Raider stood next to me, though he was sitting, tense. The other dogs had quit growling also. He was somebody she knew, but oddly, he spoke very little. A concussion made sense; I was punch drunk and wobbly on my feet, when I was standing that was. As for the shot... my shoulder hurt, throbbed, with a heat of a thousand suns. My entire body had ached when I first came to. The pain was bad now, but not as bad as it had been.

"Morphine?" a humongous man asked, stepping into my vision on the other side of Jess.

"Yeah, gave him a small dose so I could get him lashed up. You want to take an end?"

"No."

I was going to open my mouth to object, but a large knife appeared in his hand. Raider just watched. My head went back and forth between him, Jess, and the large man. The knife flicked and something underneath of me gave loose. A big hand went behind my back as he sheathed the knife, and both Jess and him worked on the bindings until she had her arms full of cordage. She started winding them up as he leaned down.

"This might hurt. Don't scream."

"Just listen to him," Jess told me, "and for God's sake, don't move."

I couldn't say anything. I was too shocked to feel myself lifted like I was a baby. Raider let out a quiet bark and ran around in a circle, his tail wagging. In front of me I could hear the other dogs also making low noises. The pain suddenly flared, and I was about to call out in pain—

A WARM WASHCLOTH WAS WIPING ME DOWN. MY EYES felt crusted shut, but when I tried to raise an arm to wipe them, I found I wasn't strong enough.

"You're awake?" Grandma asked, and I knew it was her. I'd recognize her voice anywhere.

"Grandma. How are you and Grandpa doing?" I asked.

She let out a soft chuckle and the washcloth wiped at the edge of my face.

"My eyes are gooed shut," I told her.

"Ok dear, just relax," she said, and I felt her hands gently working the washcloth over me.

First one eye, then the other opened under her care. I was in a white canvas tent by the look of things. I was laid out on what felt like a cot. I looked at my left shoulder and saw it had been gently bandaged, but my arm was in a sling and belted to my waist. I let out a deep breath. I felt about a thousand times better than I had the last time I'd passed out. A pain in my right elbow had me look that way, and I saw an IV taped in place, a bag of saline hanging from a stainless-steel hook from the framing of the tent.

"Where... Grandpa? Jess? Raider?"

It all came out in a rush.

"Everyone is fine; it was you we were worried about," she said. "Your lazy bones have been sleeping for a few days now. I was hoping you'd wake up..." her words trailed off, and she wiped her eyes.

"What do you mean?" I asked her, "I mean, wait, how long? What...?"

"You were shot almost a week ago. They removed the bullet and got your inside stitched up good but left the shoulder mostly open, so it could drain. By the time your dog and Jess found you, you had a pretty bad infection. They sedated you for a couple days, but yesterday your fever finally broke. Oh, and apparently you proposed to Duke, thinking he was Jess, while you were delirious."

"Duke? I did what?" I asked, trying to sit up. "Who is Duke?"

"Duke is the big guy who carried you out of the woods. He sat in the bed of your truck while Jess and I met up with her friends."

"Where are we?" I asked her.

"Near our homestead," Grandma said. "Grandpa's been here a couple times also, but I need him to watch after my girls. Foghorn is being a pain lately..."

"Sic Raider on Foghorn, that'll take the fight out of him," I told her with a grin.

"You just like to pick on my baby to get my hair up,"

Grandma said, trying to frown, but failing and smiling instead.

"A little bit," I admitted.

"If you weren't laid up and already had yer brains scrambled, I'd whack you one!"

I grinned as a furry shape darted inside of the tent, pushing through a loose flap. Raider started barking excitedly, spinning in a circle, jumping up and down like an excited puppy. I grinned and gave him a small wave.

"Hey buddy, what you been up to?" I asked.

"He's been watching your girlfriend and working with Yager and Diesel when he wasn't hovering over you. You scared the hell out of me. I'm reconsidering whacking you anyway. You ok with that?"

I snickered, knowing for her to act like this, it had to have scared her and she was over compensating.

"No thank you, ma'am. Why are we here and not back at the homestead?" I asked Grandma, wondering what was going on.

"You were in bad shape, and we had to work on you right away. We... couldn't get you back to our compound fast enough," Linda said, walking into the tent.

"Thank you," I told her.

"You know, you and I are going to have a talk," she said shortly, "but not right now. It's good you're awake.

Mrs. Flagg, would you like to let your husband know he's awake? I'll send some guys with you to help out."

"Nice strapping young men? Like that Carter or Jimmy?" Grandma said, an eyebrow raised.

Linda laughed. "As long as your husband doesn't mind," she said with a rueful grin.

"You take care of yourself," Grandma said, running her hands through my hair. "Looks like you're coming home soon. Not today, but soon."

Raider barked happily.

"Hey, Grandma," I called softly as she was rising to leave, she turned. "How did Raider get loose? He's the one who woke me up."

"I opened the door and told him to go find you," Grandma said, then walked out of the tent, wiping at her eyes.

Both of us watched her go. I was tired more than anything, but there was a restlessness in my body. I might not have been strong enough, but I wanted to move; I wanted to stretch and more than anything else, I wanted a bath. I felt grimy, despite Grandma washing my face with a warm washcloth. That's when Duke and Linda's husband, Dave, pushed open the flap and walked in.

"Good, he's awake," Dave said.

"Yup," Duke said.

I finally got a good look at him. He looked vaguely Samoan or Pacific Islander, but super-sized. He was almost seven feet tall if I had to guess, and his hands were the size of my face. His shoulders seemed to fill the room. Carter was a big dude, but Duke here had him beat by a third or more size and strength wise by the look of him.

"You must be Duke?" I asked.

He nodded, and I held up my good hand. I was too tired and weak to hold it up properly, but I shook his as best as I could.

"Thank you for pulling me out of there. If it hadn't been for you and Jessica..."

"You did something stupid," he said curtly, and then sat down on the stool Grandma had been using next to my cot.

The wood protested, but I think he could have as easily sat on the dirt floor and it wouldn't have made a difference. He unclipped my arm and then gently moved the strap out of the way before peeling the bandage wads back and out of the way. I looked in part curiosity and part horror at the bruised and mottled flesh on my shoulder. It had hit me in the meaty part, not the joint. Hurt like hell, but nowhere near as bad as when it had first happened. I could tell they had used iodine or something like that to keep the area clean, otherwise the bruising was in streaks.

"Healing good, the swelling is down. Seems to be draining well. How does it feel?" Duke's voice was as I remembered it—deep, rumbling.

I looked at Raider who seemed at ease with the big giant, then to Linda and Dave who had their arms crossed, watching.

"I don't know, throbbing? Not as bad as when I first woke up in the woods. My head's still sort of ringing though."

"That blow to the head could have been worse. You had a bad infection when you were found," Linda added from behind Duke, who I had to move my head to see around.

"Concussion, that and you had an infection, shock, gunshot wound that was all kinds of nasty. Boy, you should have been dead."

I bristled internally about being called 'boy' and tried to sit up more, but he gently pressed on my chest, still touching around the side of my shoulder. I winced and looked. It was angry around the edges, but I could see where sections had been stitched around the main entrance. Duke turned for a moment, getting into a box I hadn't noticed on the floor, and came back up with a handful of bandages and gauze and started re-packing my shoulder.

"What were you thinking?" Dave asked me suddenly, his voice almost a hiss, angry.

"That Duke probably ate the Stay Puft Marsh-mallow man from Ghostbusters," I said immediately, then grinned.

"Next thing you know, you're going to start calling

me the Jolly Green Giant," Duke said, though I could tell he was sort of amused.

"No, sorry. Just... Dude, I hung out with football players in college. None of them were ever... I mean..."

"Tumor as a kid. Finally got it out when I enlisted about thirty years ago. They said it'd shorten my life span if I hadn't, still might. I thought the Army life was going to do me in more than once. Now get ready, this is gonna hurt."

My eyes went wide as he put the last of the bandages on and then took my left arm and raised it ninety degrees to my body. I winced in pain, but it wasn't lightning bolts of agony. I grunted then rolled my shoulder. That hurt like a bastard, but old tendons crackled, and Duke gently lowered my arm to my side.

"What they want to know is why did you go back there alone? You blew up half the camp and burned down most of a national park." Duke's voice was serious as ever.

"Because nobody else was doing anything about it. I heard what they'd done to other women. I've seen them beat and shoot themselves. I saw that Danny guy get knifed twenty feet away from where I was hiding. If they do that stuff to their own people, what was going to happen to the women and children? You guys weren't going to help. The numbers were too over-whelming."

I was pissed, and my anger was growing, making

me strong. Duke tilted his head to the side, as if listening to a petulant child. I swear he rolled his eyes at me. That just pushed me to continue on.

"I went in trying to disable their vehicles and make enough of a ruckus that I could get the captives out of there if I could." I finished in a gasp instead of the roar I thought it would be.

Duke reached down into a bucket in front of him and came out with a washcloth and squeezed the water out with one big fist. He flicked the dripping remains on the floor and wiped my face down with it. It was humiliating in a way, but it was gentle. Like he'd done it before. Hell, he probably had. Thirty years ago? How old was this guy? He didn't look more than five or ten years older than me.

"You did a brave but stupid thing. It was practically a suicide mission. Nearly was," he said pushing it through my hair, wiping the dried sweat back off my forehead.

"Did it work?" I asked suddenly, realizing I didn't know.

In fact, when I'd last seen Jessica, she'd had blisters and her hair had been singed in a large portion. Then I remembered the charred-out trailers, and with a start, realized they were the ones I'd thought the captives were being held in.

"Yes, though we have a dozen injured, theirs and ours. Lots of bad burns. Seems you have rubbed off on

Miss Jessica. When she said that she was going back after dropping off Marshall, we had to either force her to stop and sit on her or send some men to go after her. When the bombs blew, half of their crew bugged out. The fire got pretty bad and most of the injuries happened getting the people out of the trailers. Not enough water to put it all out by the time we could gain control of the area."

"Emily and Mary?" I asked him.

"Here, waiting to talk to you. Jessica is here too, but she's kind of pissed at you," Duke said, deadpan.

Linda snorted, while Dave made a disgusted sound.

"Is that because I told you that you have the most beautiful blue eyes I've ever seen, and I wanted to stare into them until the end of time?" I asked, batting my eyelashes.

Duke laughed hard, obviously surprised. He slapped his leg, which to me sounded like a tree being snapped. His stool gave out at that point, spilling him on his butt, which made him laugh louder. Linda grinned and shook her head, but Dave stormed out, furious. It would have been a grand exit, stomping and all, but it was hard to beat a laughing giant in terms of drama. I grinned.

"You have a sense of humor. Good. I understand you're a chemist and a distiller?" he asked between chuckles that were slowly drying up.

"Chemistry by training, but yeah, basically."

"Good. We used a lot of resources on keeping you alive, stuff we can't get back."

"You want me to make you... what?" I asked him.

"Ethanol, medications, antibiotics, sedatives, bomb making materials. I assume that's what you used on the Crater gang? Home built stuff?"

"Yeah, but I wasn't too precise in my measurements. It had a little more bang than I expected," I admitted.

"I had eyes on the man holding up a jar," Linda interrupted. "One second he was there, the next... he was chunks flying fifty feet in all directions, several others as well."

"Spider?" I asked her.

"Burned but got himself out. Couldn't get a shot on him without hitting an unknown, but he got away," she answered.

"Did any of the captive women and kids get hurt?" I asked them.

"No," Duke answered for her, "almost happened though. A burning bike came down on one of the trailers, crashing through the kitchenette. There were doors at either end of the trailer. That's the one where our people got the burns." Duke's voice had softened in the telling, but I could see Linda's eyes, and she was not happy.

"So, they all escaped?" I asked.

"The gang took half of them," Linda answered, "but we were able to rescue some."

And Emily and Mary were safe. Here. Waiting. And Jessica?

"I'm tired, but my stomach is hollering that my throat's been cut," I said suddenly.

Duke chuckled and took my right arm and a piece of gauze and tape. He removed the gravity fed IV and taped a spot over the vein in my inner elbow. Then he gently, surprisingly gently, put my arm back in a sling, making sure my shoulder bandage didn't shift. He looked me over, then snorted, leaving me alone in the tent with Linda. She gave me a piercing look, then looked back at the flap before coming close.

"I appreciate what you were trying to do, but you got a lot of our people hurt," she said softly. "I won't forget that."

Her words were cold, and they felt like a bucket of ice water had been thrown on top of me. I shifted in the bed. I realized that I felt pins and needles all over; I'd been laying down for a long time. As the blood flowed, I felt a little stronger. I risked sitting up and was able to make it halfway there. Before I could crash back, Linda had an arm around my back and was pulling a pillow behind me to prop me up better.

"I feel if we're going to argue, I'll make a stronger case if I'm not stuck on my back," I told her lamely, though it was the truth.

"I'm not here to argue. The only reason our people went in was because my daughter did. If you hadn't done what you did... not to sound like a broken record but—"

"You weren't going to do anything. I'm sorry your people were hurt, but at least I did something. You guys watch and wait. Apparently, you're all set to hunker down until things are safe, but I can't ignore the horrors that are going on around here without caring. How can you?"

Raider gave me a chuff and put his head on the edge of the cot. I rubbed his big head slowly as my circulation returned and stared daggers at Linda. I was pissed; I knew people had been hurt, but people would have been hurt or worse if we'd all done nothing. They chose to get involved. I owed them my life, but I wasn't going to have them beating me over the head with it or using it as leverage. I didn't owe them any more than what they did for me, which was a lot, granted, but Duke had made it plain. He wanted a way to make medications and replace the stuff they'd used fixing me up.

I technically could do what they wanted with the supplies and proper equipment, but I didn't really know how to go about it. I had focused more on industrial instead of other applications of chemistry when I was going to college, but my mind was trying to do too many things at once. That's when I noticed Linda's face turning beet red. My words had struck home, and she was either furious or—

"You bastard," she said softly, a large tear running down her face, "don't you ever accuse me of not caring!"

I waited, my mind reeling as her chest hitched and she sat down hard on the floor next to me. Her whole body shook as she started sobbing, one arm leaned against the cot by my feet, covering her face.

"What's going on?" Linda's husband, Dave, walked in.

I shrugged. "She read me the riot act, and I gave her some truth."

I saw the tent flap open again and another figure step in. Things were about to get busy, and Raider gave out a low warning growl, his muscles going rigid under my right hand as I continued to pet him. I waited. A moment later, a blistered Jessica moved out from behind her father who was kneeling next to Linda.

"I'm ok," Linda said, "I'm just not as much of a monster as you make me out to be," she said, looking at me, her face tear streaked.

I felt ashamed suddenly, and Jessica's eyes followed her mom, then looked up at me.

"I'm sorry your people got hurt," I told the room at large, "but I didn't ask anybody to come after me. I would have died if it hadn't been for Duke and Jessica, but that was a price I was willing to pay. One man's life, if it meant saving ten or fifteen others. I was willing and ready to pay it."

"Twenty-three and a half," Jessica said.

"What?" I asked, turning my attention to her.

Raider calmed at her voice and sat down on his hind end. It was a pain to reach him, so I pushed myself up with my good arm.

"Twenty-three and a half women and children. That's how many we got from the trailers and into the bushes before the gang organized and got the rest."

"A half?" I asked.

"Apparently, one of the gals we got out is six months pregnant. Unless it's twins, I'm only counting half a head until the baby bump is born," Jess said.

Her face was tight, and I didn't know if it was anger or pain. The blisters I'd noticed when I was being dragged out had drained and were scabbed, her beautiful hair was half burned off on one side, and she had a long streak on her arm that was still blistered, as if she'd brushed up against something hot. All in all, she looked fantastic still.

"Is she ok? Is her baby ok?" I asked.

"Wes," Linda said, getting up and wiping her eyes, "I have half a mind to let you have it, but I can see why my daughter's fallen so hard for you. You weren't shot horribly, but the wound grew infected, and you had a concussion that left you unconscious off and on for days. The shock and infection almost killed you anyway, and some of the first words out of your mouth are to ask how everyone else is doing?"

"The boy has some cajones," Dave said quietly, "but you can't blame us for the inaction. It could have easily gone the other way. We could have all died, so could have you."

I looked away as Jess nodded in agreement with her father. Again, it was a price I was willing to pay.

"So, you're saying Jess has a thing for me?" I asked them.

Linda let out a bark of laughter, wiping her eyes. Dave grimaced and shook his head at me. I looked at Jess who just rolled her eyes skyward.

"Mom, Dad, there are a couple people outside who want to see Wes, and Mom, you're wanted by communications. Scouts have an urgent message for you."

"How bad?" Linda asked, suddenly sober.

"Bad. We are going to have to move, but they think we have time to hunt a hole."

"On it," Dave said.

"You and I aren't finished," Linda said, standing up.

"For now, we are," I shot back.

She rolled her eyes this time and turned and stalked out. I could tell she wanted to stomp the way Dave had earlier. How much of this was real, how much an act? I couldn't tell. The only thing constant I could trust was sitting next to me, my hand scratching behind his ears.

"How are you?" I asked Jessica as we were suddenly alone.

"I'm pretty good, all in all," she said, motioning to her face and arms where the scabs from the burns were evident.

"You look good," I told her.

She snorted and walked over, pushing my eyelids up. Raider sat up taller, watching her intently.

"Don't worry, I'm not going to make him cry," she told my dog, "this time," She finished under her breath.

"Concussion seems to be gone. They say you have to take it easy for a week or two afterward, but yours was pretty severe. Say two to three weeks. And I do not look good; half my hair caught fire trying to find you."

She sat down on the floor next to me, noting the crushed stool next to the cot and she raised an eyebrow artfully.

"Duke," I told her lamely.

"Ahh, yeah, he's a big guy. When he joined the group, we had a ton of people who were quietly begging us to be sure he had enough food for himself and then some."

"How are you?" I asked her again.

"I'm fine," she said, pushing her hands through my hair until a sharp pain had me wince.

"Ouch," I said, flinching away from her grip.

"I'm just checking the stitches," she said.

"Stitches?" I asked.

"Whatever hit you in the head cut your scalp open. You had bone showing. Our doc cleaned you up and stitched you closed. I told him you were never that pretty to begin with, so it didn't matter if—"

She squeaked as I reached over and poked her in the side. She rolled her eyes again and gave me a smile.

"What's coming? You mentioned something about communications and timing?"

"Remember me taking Marshall to our people?" she asked me.

I nodded, remembering the fishing jokes and Grandpa's lewd commentary.

"Lance's people have picked sides. Lance now works for Spider directly, judging by radio intercepts we've gotten. They pretend they still have Marshall, but he's safe with us. Apparently, Spider has people. A lot of people. Hard to imagine in Arkansas that there were this many criminal masterminds but..."

Her words trailed off and I brushed my hand through her hair, careful not to hit the scabs and healing blisters. She moaned softly and leaned in. I ran my hands through her hair, marveling that with the world ending, I was making a move on my new girlfriend.

"How many? And are they coming this way?" I asked her.

"Apparently there's close to a hundred more men,

and the numbers seem to grow as they're heading south from the larger cities. People are throwing in with them because they have food, medication, drugs, and safety. The big cities are emptying out of people FEMA missed, and there's a certain type of person that seems to gravitate to men like Spider."

"If they've survived this long without starving or from revenge killings, they're pretty rough guys?" I asked her.

"Yes," she said softly, "and there's quite a few of them who were military and have been making coded radio contacts with what appears to be a large force."

"What?" I said, sitting up and wincing at the pain.

"Hold still or you're going to rip yourself open," she said roughly.

I sat back as much as I could and tried to relax. The jolt of pain had made me start sweating hard, and I noticed my backpack on the floor next to Raider.

"Ok, get my pack for me, would you?" I asked her.

"Sure," she said and lifted it up, putting it in my lap.

I got the canteen out of it and swished it around, smiling at the heft of it.

"What are you doing?" she asked as I started unscrewing the cap.

I took a slug of Grandma's doctored lemonade. It was warm, but it lit a fire in my stomach after I had four or five fast swallows. I handed it to Jessica, who sniffed it, then took a sip. Her eyes went wide in surprise.

"I was going to call this our second date?" I asked lamely.

"One of these days, we're going to have us a real date," she grinned, taking another long slow sip.

The flap of the tent parted, and two feminine figures stepped in. I recognized them both immediately.

"Is he awake yet?" Mary asked quietly.

"Yes, you want to talk to him?" Jess asked the little girl, her voice tender and shaking.

"Yes please," she said, her little hand in her mother's.

As they stepped forward, I saw the tear-streaked face of Emily.

"You warned us. I'm sorry you got hurt but thank you!" Emily said, dropping her daughter's hand and leaning down kissing me on the forehead.

Jessica made a rude sound and Raider made a chuffing, sneezing sound. When Emily stood back, I rubbed at the spot a moment. She looked at me tenderly with something else I couldn't pinpoint.

"This time, Mister Wes, I have candy for you," Mary told me, pressing a Hershey's into my hand.

Raider chuffed loudly, then licked her suddenly before letting out a quick bark.

14

WITH ME AWAKE, things started happening fast. After the ladies left Jessica alone with Raider and I, they started packing up. The tent was taken down around us as I was fed first some broth, then what tasted to me like Dinty Moore Beef Stew. I could feel myself getting stronger, and my stomach began cramping. I couldn't tell if it was from hunger, or from too much food after almost a week of nothing but liquids. I needed it. I sipped water after Jess took my doctored lemonade away. I'd humor her for now. I had a stash in my pack if her group hadn't removed it.

The frame of the tent was being packed into a pickup truck, then the canvas folded. All the while I was sitting on a cot. Yager and Diesel sat nearby, as still as statues, watching all of us. Vicious at command, but wonderful companions when not on a job. Lastly, I was helped to my feet and put into the passenger side of the truck. I was about to object when I felt the bed of the truck move. I looked back and saw Raider had hopped in with both of Jessica's dogs.

"Where are we going?" I asked, not sure where we were.

It looked like an overgrown field, but we were surrounded by trees. Not an area I'd hunted in, though it was vaguely familiar.

"Back to our facility," Jess said. "Carter hasn't medically released you entirely."

"What's Duke do for you guys?" I asked as she fired up my truck and put it in gear.

"He's got some medical training, but mostly, he's... Our go-to guy when things get hairy."

"How come I hadn't met him before?" I asked her.

"He's... quiet. Does a lot of our observation work. He's like a ghost when he wants to be. I couldn't find you and neither could he. If it hadn't been for Raider..."

Her words trailed off. I was horribly weak, and the seatbelt was rubbing against my left arm. I adjusted it for more comfort and watched slowly as Jessica pulled onto the road and worked the gearshift like she'd been driving trucks forever.

"Hey, aren't we on the old lumber—"

"Shhhh," she said, her hand patting my leg.

I tried to ignore how casual that move was, and I

realized as she hushed me, she had an earwig in her right ear and was listening to something. Dammit, why couldn't she have just put the radio on the dash and let us both listen? As much as I wanted to watch, pay attention, I felt myself drifting to sleep. The food had done much to restore me, but I was tired. I felt a hand against my chest and opened my eyes to see Jess grinning at me.

"Didn't want you to bump your head on the dash," she said as the entire truck bounced across an unseen rut.

We'd turned down a two track at some point, and I recognized this from the time Grandpa and I had gone to enlist their help.

"I'm good," I said, scooting back and straightening up in the seat. "How long was I out?"

"Twenty-minute nap. You snore, you know that?"

"I do not," I said, but I was grinning.

"What's that smirk for?" she asked.

I shook my head, remembering the night in the barn. She snored too, but I wasn't going to fill her in on that tidbit. She snorted at me, and I glanced in the rearview. Three big fuzzy heads were staring through the back glass. I thought about opening the middle window up, but I knew Raider would crawl through and make a pain of himself. If Diesel tried to follow... we'd have a hard time. I was actually surprised that they'd stayed in the back of the truck without complaint.

Another thirty yards, we made a turn onto what looked like a natural opening between the new growth of trees. Jess pulled to a stop in the middle and tossed the keys on the narrow dash.

"This is it," she said. "Don't move and let me come around to let you out."

"I'm not that weak," I protested.

"It's a security thing," she whispered.

I nodded and waited, remembering the protocols she'd talked about when she'd been prepping Marshall days back. I was able to get my seat belt off as she got out. She lowered the tailgate, and I felt rather than saw the dogs jump down. I heard Diesel let out a low woof. For some reason, the big slab of dog meat reminded me of something. I cracked my door just as Jess made it to my side. She opened it and offered me an arm. I grinned and swung my legs out. They immediately turned to Jell-O and she let out a surprised shout, ducking lower than me and putting her shoulder under my armpit and using her legs to push me back up.

"Owwwww," I grumbled softly as my head and shoulder banged on the door frame.

"Shhh, big baby," she chided.

"Step to the left," a voice called out.

"I can't, he's not steady enough on his feet."

"The tree of liberty..." the voice called.

I knew this one! I almost opened my mouth, but Jess beat me to it. "Is used to hang the traitors from," she finished, not even remotely close to the quote I'd thought of.

It hit me, it was a pass phrase? Something like a duress code? If she'd answered any other way, I probably would have had my head splattered all over my upholstery. Several figures stepped into the open, one of them I recognized. The medic was looking me over, shaking his head.

"How's the shoulder?" he asked me.

"Not too bad," I said, looking around.

There were four men including Carter and a lady who looked to be Grandma's age, though quite a bit wirier and mean looking. All were dressed in Mossy Oak and boonie hats, except for the lady. Her steely silver hair was tied in a severe bun. She gave me a hard stare, then approached me. Carter stepped back, and she got up in my face. She had to tilt her head up to look at me, but I met her glare. Jess repositioned her hands, and I was able to stand a bit straighter. She grabbed my chin and moved my head side to side, then tilted it so she could see my scalp. Then she gently pushed the sleeve of my t-shirt back and felt the flesh on the outside of the bandages. I tried not to wince at her firm grip, but I could see my flesh was angry, bruised looking. Then she let me go and stared me in the eyes again.

"You're a dumbass," she said and turned, walking back the way she'd come, a .45 on her right hip.

"I... Thank you?!" I said over her shoulder.

"How bad are you feeling?" Carter asked.

"Still wobbly on my feet," I admitted.

"That blow to the head almost killed you," he said, taking Jess' spot, and put an arm around my back, grabbing my belt. "We're going to walk slow."

"But my—"

Raider barked happily. He'd come around the other side of the truck and was lined up with his two new best friends. Yager and Diesel were on either side of him. *Traitor.*

"I've got your stuff. Carter will help you, and the dogs..." Jess said something in German and both Yager and Diesel laid down.

Raider looked at both of them, then back at me before laying down. Jess pulled a leash out of her back pocket and walked to my dog, clipping it on him.

"You walk with me, buddy," she said, patting him on the head. "My boys know the trails."

"Oh, ok," I mumbled, my muscles starting to strain from being upright.

I was weaker than I'd thought, and was a little bit startled to hear Carter say it was my head that had almost done me in. No way. That couldn't be?

"One last thing," a man who'd been sitting back said, pulling out what looked like a black scrap of cloth. He fluffed it out and I realized it was a hood, one with no eye holes, just a slit for my mouth, "Put this on."

"Henry, dammit, I—"

"No arguments, Jess," the man she'd called Henry said, "or he can go sit at home with his family."

"He needs us to recover, and we need him to show us how to—"

"Not here, not now. Don't breach security and don't you ever question me again in front of others."

"Yes, sir," she said quietly.

I was halfway awed at the way Jess reacted and halfway pissed enough to want to knock the lights out of this guy. I took a closer look at Henry who appeared to be somewhere between his mid to late forties to a little older. Wiry, hard. Mean eyes. That described half the men down here in the hollers though, but he had some authority, and nobody was speaking up or out for Jessica. I'd thought Jessica's family was sort of the top of the food chain in this group. I had another thing coming.

"I'll do it," I said, holding out my hand.

Carter propped me up and helped me get the hood on and positioned. I never could have done it myself one handed and remained upright, something Carter seemed to have intuited.

"Thanks," I told him quietly as he got under my shoulder again, to lend me his strength.

"Don't mention it," he whispered back, "and just a tip, don't mouth off to Henry."

"Who is he?" My voice was almost too low for anybody else to hear.

"The real guy in charge," he whispered back.

WE HAD TO STOP OFTEN FOR ME TO REST AND FOR Carter to push a straw into my mouth to drink. It was hot under the hood. I couldn't see out of it, but when the cloth moved just right, I could get a glimpse of the grass and what looked like a well-worn trail. Nobody talked except Jessica reassuring Raider, but I heard a series of clicks on the radio from someone in front of Carter and me.

We came to a halt, and I felt something brush my leg. I put my hand down and Raider's wet nose pressed into my hand, then gave me a reassuring lick. I felt around and patted him on the head. Another dog, probably Yager, sniffed my hand, then pressed his head under it, pushing Raider back. I scratched his ears. I could tell it wasn't Diesel, his head was shaped differently, and he was definitely the larger of the three canines.

"Can he climb down a ladder?" Henry asked.

"He's got use of one arm, and he's wobbly on his feet," Jessica said from slightly to the side of me.

Being blindfolded wasn't all it was cracked up to be. I turned my head as if to follow the conversation, but realized I was all but invisible to them. A non-entity.

"Do you think you can climb down a steel ladder?" Carter asked me softly. "I can go first if needed and steady you."

"I'm not sure," I admitted. "Today's the first day I've been on my feet, and I feel like we've gone on for twenty miles."

Sweat was running off of me; part of it was the radiating pain in my shoulder, the other part was the heat and exertion.

"We can't afford for him to get stuck—" Henry's voice was cut off by a deep one.

"If he can't make it, I'll carry him if needed. Ain't no sense taking him the long way when he's ready to pass out already."

Duke, I'd recognize his voice anywhere.

Where did he come from? He hadn't been with us, hadn't driven with Jess and I, and I hadn't seen him come up.

"I got a better idea," Jess said.

"What?" a few of them chorused.

"Let's get him on the material slide, rope him down slow using a safety sling. If it's good enough for our dry goods, it should work for him. If he'll fit," she finished that by patting my arm. At least I thought it was her.

"Slide?" I asked.

"It's a narrow opening but made out of sheet metal riveted together. No sharp edges. It's got a pretty sharp incline, but in a harness and with Duke and I holding the ropes, you should be fine. Easier than climbing, right?" Carter's voice sounded upbeat, maybe even happy that they'd found a better solution.

"I don't care," I said, my legs close to buckling again. "Where are my grandparents?" I asked them.

"Back at the homestead," Carter's voice said from my other side. "We can't bring them here, and you're still too busted up to be there without somebody watching over you."

"I got my bell rung. A few days of rest and food and I should be good to –"

"No, you're not. We kept you sedated because we weren't sure how much of the brain swelling had gone down. Didn't want you to hurt yourself. It's common in TBIs in the early days. I'm frankly shocked you're able to stand at all right now."

TBI?

"I should be there with them, ready to help in case..."

"If Lance and Spider's boys come back, we have people in place to take them into hiding. They are being well watched over," Henry's voice came from ahead of me. "Let's get him in the harness."

I'D GOTTEN A BRIEF LOOK AROUND BEFORE THE ROPE WAS clipped to the harness. There was a section on the side of what looked to be a drop off of a tree lined area that had been cleared out. Camouflage netting was woven with natural materials and was pulled back, showing what looked like two man hole covers. One was set at an angle into what looked like stone, the other a few feet away, went straight down. There were heavy locks on each. Duke had produced a key and pulled the lid off like it weighed nothing.

"There's easier ways in, but it's a longer walk," he said by way of explanation.

"Let's go. Jess should be in place," Henry said impatiently.

I FELT LIKE I WAS BEING LOWERED DOWN AN INCLINED laundry chute. My back and legs were almost flat on the sheet metal, and I felt like I might have shot down at speeds a roller coaster would envy if it weren't for the rope and the harness around my legs and waist. I could hear Carter and Duke, both large men, talking as they lowered me. Jessica's voice floated up from below occasionally, calling out now and then to make sure I was still conscious and awake.

"Your feet are almost at the bottom," Jess said.

I tensed, and then I was free of the chute, the harness digging into my hips a bit. I held on with my good arm until I got my legs under me. It was pitch black, but I felt Jess' hands as she felt for the rope and unclipped me.

"All good," she said into her radio.

I wondered how it was working; I felt like I'd gone fifty feet straight down into the rock.

The rope started coming down the chute behind me and I took an uneasy step forward, my hand finding Jessica's shoulder. She pulled me close, hugging me. My legs were giving out, so she helped me down to the ground.

"I was so worried you weren't going to make it," she said softly, "you shouldn't even be on your feet."

"Then why move me?" I asked, feeling dizzy, nauseous again.

"We didn't have a choice. The men coming to join up with Spider will have this entire valley covered soon."

"I'm worried about my family," I told her softly.

"I'm worried for all of us," she replied, her hand going through my hair gently.

I winced as her fingers found the stitches, and she

used the tip of a finger to feel it. She pulled her hand back in gloom and rubbed her fingertips together, seeing if I had been bleeding again?

"Why can't my family come here?" I asked her.

"Henry's decision," she said softly, "and I lost the argument."

"I thought you and your parents were the head of this outfit?" I asked, confused.

"We sort of are," she said softly, "but Henry is the reason we're all here and ready. He started the MAG years and years back, before we were born."

"MAG?" I asked.

"Mutual Assistance Group. You'll find out anyway, but in this area, we have a dozen and a half or so families. My parents and I live in this location, where others are spread out. Not everyone is underground, but this is the group's fallback location."

I couldn't make out anything but her in the gloom, but somewhere a small light was blinking. It wasn't bright enough to illuminate everything, but I could pinpoint it now that my eyes had adjusted.

"What is this place?" I asked her.

"It used to be a communications bunker—"

"Bunker?" I asked her, surprised.

"Not like you think. 'Ma Bell has these all over the country from when they had the big old computers to run the old phone lines in the seventies and eighties. When the area was upgraded, this place was decommissioned and abandoned. The lumber companies in this area never use it, and we sort of cleaned it out and took it for ours. The way in is almost impassable unless you come in on foot."

"Something about being dug into the hillside?" I asked, stretching, remembering an old conversation.

"Something like that," she whispered as a flashlight lit up at the far end and a happy bark greeted me.

15

I HAD PASSED out again or fell asleep. I didn't remember which. I found myself laying on what felt like a canvas topped cot. A small candle was burning on a wooden produce crate that was stood on end. My head felt like a rung bell, and my eyes like they had been scooped out and replaced with crushed glass. The headache I'd had earlier was nothing like the one I had right now. I rolled on my right side, listening to the cot squeak, pulling the rough wool blanket half off me. My left arm was still in a sling, but I could make out in the candle-light that my shirt had been removed and fresh bandages were put on. A low woof sounded outside a louvered door.

"Is he awake?" a feminine voice asked.

Two excited barks and claws scratching the door answered whoever asked. It didn't sound like Jessica, but it looked like I was going to find out as the door opened. I squinted as brighter light blinded me. I held up a hand as a figure walked in the door, my dog rushing ahead of her, before a smaller figure followed.

"It's ok, Wes," she said, "It's Emily."

"And it's me, Mary, and your doggy, Raider!" the short figure said happily.

I tried to sit up, but the world swam. Raider pushed his head under my hand, and I started scratching his ears as my eyes adjusted to the light.

"Where are we?" I asked her, trying to sit up again.

Emily hurried to my side, pushing my dog back with a hand and wrapped her arms around me. I could feel her thin figure against my bare chest as she used her upper body strength to lift me more or less into a sitting position. I helped as much as I could, until I had my back against what felt like a block wall. Both of us were breathing hard from the effort, and I realized something. I could see and smell that she'd recently bathed. No longer was she the grimy and dirty woman I'd first met. Instead, she was dressed in clean clothing and looked pretty. She backed up, pushing her hair out of her face and blew out the candle. Maybe to prevent all of us from knocking it over? Now that my eyes had adjusted, I could see that the room I was in was barely six feet by eight feet, and there was an LED light on the low ceiling outside my room.

"Momma says you're in the closet, but someday you're going to come out," Mary said.

My eyes must have shown my surprise, because Emily snickered.

"What?" I asked her, feeling something stir within me.

"This used to be a storage closet," Emily said by way of explanation. "In case you were sick, they kept you away from the others. Kind of like quarantine."

"Oh, ok," I said, rocking forward.

Raider put his head across my legs in a hug, then turned and walked to the doorway, making a low whining sound.

"Your doggy has to go to the potty," Mary said. "I'll take him to Miss Jessica."

"I... ok?" My thinking was slow, and my thoughts were confused. Hungover, that's what I felt like.

"After they got you down here, you passed out. We kept waking you up to feed you, but whatever they are giving you makes you sleepy. It's been two days."

Morphine, I remembered Jess saying she'd given me a small dose when they moved me. Had they done it again?

"Oh, ok. Where's Jess?" I asked, instantly regretting it as I saw a hurt look come across Emily's face.

"She's outside working with her dogs."

"Oh, ok. I'm surprised to see you two here," I told her.

She sat down on the floor, her legs going under the cot next to mine and she put her elbows on the bed, her chin on her hands.

"I had nowhere else to go. My husband's grandpa is dead, my sister-in-law's gone with the kids."

"Were they captured?" I asked in surprise.

"I doubt it," she said softly. "They had a plan of where to go, and we all made a pact that if one of us didn't make it, we'd take the kids and bug out to an old fishing shack."

"Oh, they aren't there?" I asked, curious and hoping they'd all made it away from Spider's crew.

"I don't know where it is. I'm a recent member of the family, if you consider I married the youngest of the boys seven years ago."

"And I went and—"

"Don't," she said, looking up and putting a gentle hand across my lips. "He made his choices a long time ago, and to be honest, I'm sort of glad he's gone."

I was shocked. It must have been the drugs. That had to be the drugs. I'd probably killed her husband, and she was happy—

She pulled up her shirt, exposing part of her bra. I was going to look away, but I saw a line of scars on her side, round, like bullet holes. Dozens of them. I stared, and then reached out with my good hand and touched one. It was raised and the size of a pencil eraser in diameter. She shivered, and I snatched my hand back, realizing what I was doing. She pulled her shirt down, covering them.

"He liked to hurt me, burn me with cigarettes. Said my screams got him off," she said, meeting my gaze.

"He abused you."

She nodded. "At first, I played along, thinking that's what a good wife was supposed to do, but the little things became bigger things, then worse things, until he was burning me and beating me. If I hadn't come down here for his father's funeral, I would have had filed for divorce already. If... the country hadn't gone to hell, that is."

I didn't know what to say.

"And then you come along. My daughter was half delirious with happiness when you gave her a candy bar and food, and you told me my husband was dead. I could have wept for joy, but my sisters-in-law... their marriages weren't the hell that mine was."

"I'm sorry," I said lamely.

In the distance, I heard a door slam, and I pulled the blanket a little bit closer to me.

"Don't be," she said, taking my hand in hers. "I just wanted to say thank you, again. You saved us more than once. I don't think I can ever repay you properly."

The last bit was said with a grin and being a guy, I thought of a couple of ways she might repay me but squashed that right away. Jessica had my heart, and the drugs must have been making me a bit loopy. Attraction happens, but it didn't mean you had to act on it, and I wasn't smitten with Emily the way I was with Jess. I let her hand go to scratch my face where an itch had developed.

"Somebody had to keep an eye on you, and Carter is busy watching the others, so I volunteered."

"Thank you," I said, wondering how I had lost so much time. "Is there a restroom anywhere around here?"

"Yes, do you think you can stand?" she asked me.

"I don't know," I said honestly.

"Well, come on," she said, pulling her legs out and standing, offering me her arms.

I took them and was surprised at how much stronger I felt once I made it to my feet. I wobbled a bit, but the small woman wrapped her arms around me, almost like she was trying to hug the life out of me.

"Ready?" she asked as I breathed heavily.

"Yeah," I said, one arm around her shoulder.

———

I USED THE BATHROOM AND SHOWERED ON MY OWN. I marveled that the bunker had running water. It wasn't hot, but more room temperature, which wasn't very warm either. It seemed to be a constant sixty-five degrees, though I didn't hear a furnace going anywhere. I remembered that the ground temperatures stayed constant, but knew an air exchange had to happen so mold and mildew didn't develop. A mystery for another day. Getting dressed though…

"Just let me help you, dammit," Emily said from the other side of the bathroom door.

The bathroom had a bench, two shower stalls with a handicapped chair, two free-standing toilets with a dividing will between them, and two sink basins. It was almost commercial, like an upgraded truck stop bathroom.

"I got this," I said, trying to get one leg through my pants.

"Who do you think cleaned you up while you were out cold?"

"You?" I asked.

"Yes. So, open the door before you open the wound in your shoulder up, or fall and hit your head. I've seen it all already."

The bench was beside the door, and I looked in frustration at the sweatpants I was trying to put on. I'd almost done it but had turned one leg inside out. Having only one arm to do things while feeling dizzy wasn't helping. At least I'd gotten my boxers on myself. Reluctantly, I turned the handle, unlocking it at the same time. Emily came in and pushed me upright gently.

"Seriously, you shouldn't be doing this on your own," she scolded.

"I've been getting dressed, going to the bathroom, and showering on my own, all my life."

"Maybe you should try showering with others," Jess said from the doorway as Emily was straightening out the pant leg I'd turned inside out.

"You volunteering?" I asked her, looking up and smiling.

She grinned and walked in, letting the door close behind her.

"Absolutely," she said, kissing me on the head. "Emily, thank you for everything."

"I've almost got it..." Then she pulled my waist, and I stood up with both legs in the correct pant legs.

"This is awkward," I told Jess, who just grinned and shook her head. "She's been—"

"Oh she knows," Emily told me.

Knows what exactly? I pulled the pants up.

"We've been taking turns watching you and sitting by your door," Jessica explained.

I heard a demonic sounding woof that seemed to shake the floor from outside the bathroom. The sound echoed around the tiled room. Jess backed up and cracked the door. Diesel pushed his way inside and headed straight for me. He was rumbling in a low way that made me break out in goose flesh. He pushed Jessica aside with his greater bulk and I sat down, backing up to protect my vitals, my hands in front of me to ward off an attack.

He pushed his head into my hands, then turned his head, licking me and rubbing his face all over my hands and legs. I sat there as he made that low rumbling sound.

"Dogs have glands on their face. Diesel here is marking you as one of his pack."

"His pack?" I asked.

"He thinks he's in charge here. Sometimes, we go along with it," Jess said with a grin as Emily patted the big dog's flank and scratched his back.

Diesel's head was almost the size of a basketball, and I put my hands on the side of his head and rubbed his face. His rumble was louder, and he pushed me in the side. I grunted in pain as my left arm was moved.

"That's enough," Jess said to him, smacking him on the rump. "Wes, let's get your shirt on and take you for a tour."

"Sure," I said, looking at the shirt that was left for me.

It was a white Hanes undershirt, a tank top. In another life I would have called it a wife beater. I held it up in one hand and saw Emily watching me. She grinned, shrugging her shoulders. She got the reference without me saying anything. It made sense though; it would keep fabric off my shoulder. I pulled it on with the help of the ladies and, when they helped me up, I felt better still. The shower had done wonders for me, though I suspected the effect was mostly mental.

"Let me show you our place," Jess said, putting an arm under my good shoulder. "Thank you, Emily. Is it ok if Mary plays with the dogs?" she asked the shorter woman who was on my left side, her arm around my waist.

"Of course," Emily told us, giving me a wave. "Let me know when you need a hand or need me to take over, so you can get some rest." She let me go, and I was standing on my own.

"I will," Jess told her.

"I think I can walk on my own now."

"You can't fall and hit your head, Wes."

Her words hit me funny, and I grinned.

"What's so funny? You cheating death, or scaring me half dead?"

"No, it's... It's stupid. Never mind."

Emily had turned left out of the doorway, and I followed slowly, pulling the door open.

"Try me."

"Grandpa's buddy is Lester Doyle. Me and him... growing up... He'd always say, "Hey, Wes" and I'd say, "Hey, Les", and now that I have you in my life it's, "Hey, Jess"."

She shook her head and put an arm around me as we walked slowly. The corridor was short and opened up into a larger room I'd seen earlier. We passed the door to my closet ten feet from the opening.

"Yeah, that is sorta dumb," she said, tickling my left side, "but it's funny too. In a way."

"So, tell me about this place."

IT HAD ONCE HOUSED COMPUTERS AND A WAY TO energize or power the old phone systems. The original purpose wasn't a nuclear hardened shelter, but one that was away from the elements. Places like these had been built all over the country to house equipment. Building it underground gave a natural method to keep the computers and generators cool. Because of that, the facility had its own water catchment, filtration, and septic systems. Jessica's father had left much of the largest equipment in place and sold the rest for scrap to fund their prepping. I marveled that places like this even existed. Supposedly if a trunk of phone lines went down, a team would work here on re-routing or reconnecting things, so communications always went through, hence the reason they had bathrooms, water, etc.

"Where does the power come from?" I asked, noting that what lighting there was, was sparse but bright.

"Solar panels hidden near the top of the rock pile,"

Jess said, leading me to the center of the semi-circular room where several couches were pulled into a rough triangle, "but most of it comes from hydroelectric. We have a couple setups running from an artesian well spring. It's not much, not enough to run more than lights, but it's what we have."

"I'm glad for it," I said, marveling at the difference in the light.

I'd gotten used to candle and alcohol lamp light, but the harsh bright white of the LEDs was comforting.

"It isn't much, it's a little cold... but..."

I looked around the semi-circular room and saw a line of doors and pointed, about to ask about them.

"Bedrooms and storage," she said. "It was a spot that was mostly free of equipment. Dad knocked together some walls for privacy, put in some doors... We sort of have the emergency fall back location of everyone in the group."

"How come nobody else claimed it first? My grandpa said a group has been in this area for decades."

"Timing. When they built this place in the late sixties, early seventies, guys like Henry already had their own spots built up. When it was abandoned in the 90s when fiber optic started getting popular, we were worried the land around here was going to be sold. That's when Henry subleased it from the lumber company for a fishing camp. Supposedly a twenty- or thirty-year land lease, but we had to concede access, so they could get to the rest of the state land."

"But how did you end up with a sweet ass bunker right out of *Doomsday Preppers*?" I asked, a hint of amusement coloring my words.

"Lucky," Jess said, letting me sit on one of the couches.

They weren't comfortable like the ones we had at home, and I realized it was home built and uphol-stered. Probably the only way to do things, this remote. I saw several furry streaks and heard Mary's laugh, then the pounding of feet with a murmur of voices. Yager and Raider jumped over the back of the couch next to Jessica as the back of it got rocked, and I got a big tongue on the back of the head. I turned, and Diesel gave me another kiss on the side of the face. I wiped it off as Mary ran up to us, red faced.

"My momma said to tell you that your momma said that dinner is ready."

"Oh good," Jessica said. "You want to eat outside, or in here?"

"First things first," I asked her, "How's my grand-parents?" I felt guilty for not asking before now, but I was way out of my element.

"Good, last I heard. I think Jimmy has sore ribs from laughing at your grandparents' antics."

"They are a hoot. I wish Raider could stick with

them," I said, watching him turn to look at me as he heard his name.

"We thought about that while you were in the canvas tent, but he didn't want to leave your side. Your grandma said he needed you, so she never took him back."

"Yeah," I said, "I still wish..." I let my words trail off.

I hadn't seen my grandpa at all since I'd said my goodbye, with the whole 'just in case' awkwardness. I wished I could see him, talk to him.

"Mister Wes," Mary said loudly, surprising me. I'd forgotten she'd run up behind Diesel.

"Hiya, kiddo." I looked her over. She was clean and in fresh, new-looking clothing, her hair braided loosely.

"Did my candy bar help?" she asked, being serious.

"I think so?" I said, not sure if I'd ended up eating it or not; there were lots of gaps in my memory.

"Good," she said and hugged my good shoulder from behind me and then took off.

Raider let out a chuff and jumped over the couch and started chasing her. She let out a laughing squeal, only to be followed by both dogs that had waited behind. We both turned and watched as she ran in a circle in the room, avoiding the dogs. I knew Raider could have ran her down, but he stayed just far enough behind her to keep her running fast. Yager and Diesel kept pace with Raider, each nipping at each other and barking happily.

"This place is huge," I told her.

"This is the lower level. That staircase," she pointed to a metal staircase that went up and turned out of sight, "leads up to the main level. It looks like they stored extra stuff there, but that's the main door in and out. It used to have more of a flat approach to the main door, but we took care of that."

"Took care of that?" I asked, watching as the girl made another lap.

"Yeah, we blasted part of the rock face, taking out part of the hill to make the approach more difficult. It was risky, but it worked, and the loggers never come near here. In fact, it wouldn't surprise me if they've forgotten about it."

"We can hope," I said as Raider broke off the chase and walked over to me, his tail wagging, his whole body moving in his excitement.

I pet him as I heard a door bang shut somewhere.

"Sounds like Emily is back," Jess said, shooting me a look and then poking me in the ribs.

"I'm a guy, and I'm usually pretty blind to things, but..."

"Oh, I know. We've actually talked about that," Jess said, a mischievous smile on her face.

"And...?" I asked, wondering if I was in trouble, or if there was going to be a jealousy thing going on.

"She can't help how she sort of feels, and you have this habit of charging in, trying to save damsels in distress. She knows you and I have this thing... but she teased me that I better not mistreat you, because she'd be ready to snatch you away."

"It's... Lord, I thought I could have been wrong. I feel sorta stupid for asking," I said softly as Mary slowed down, though both Yager and Diesel still followed her.

"No, it's pretty obvious. I felt awkward when she insisted on being the one to look after you, but then she showed me the scars."

"Yeah, she showed me too," I said and watched her eyebrows shoot up to her hairline. "Right here on her side," I said, pointing nearer to the waist.

"They're all up her side, back, back of the legs..." she whispered as Mary was coming close, "but not all cigarette burns. I guess he used to beat her with his belt. A spanking fetish that turned dark and left marks. She said you'd saved her from her husband, as well as those men at the park."

"She said she had been planning on leaving her husband anyway," I whispered back as she got close to me.

"Are you two going to start making out?" Mary asked suddenly.

"Maybe..." I looked at her.

"Ewww. Come on Raider, let's go upstairs and find the ball."

All three dogs' ears perked up at that and then Raider looked at me, head tilted.

"I don't mind, but you have to stay close to her. Go ahead and have some fun."

Raider made a grumbling sound deep in his chest, then rubbed his head against my leg before turning to the little girl. They started up the stairs but stopped as three people walked down from what had to be a landing between floors. Emily was in front, followed by Linda and Dave. The latter two wore camouflage and carried their guns. That made me think of the room I'd woken up in. I'd seen my pack, but not my guns. My pistol could have been in my backpack, but I doubted it. Unless they'd sent it back with Grandma?

"Hey, he's up," Dave said, seeing me.

"And he isn't stinking up the joint anymore," Emily said, a spring in her step.

"She's so stinking happy it's making my teeth ache," Jessica said in a low voice, her lips barely moving.

"Jealous?" I asked her.

She put her arm around my waist and leaned in, kissing me hard. I kissed her back but was careful. The way I was turned made the skin pull tight around my left shoulder. Her breath caught, and I ran my hands through her hair briefly. She let out a laugh around my lips when I got to the singed part that had been trimmed off.

"Hey, you two," Emily said, "I think you're about to have some visitors."

I broke away and turned, able to make it to my feet on my own for the first time.

"Hey, guys, thank you. For everything," I said, holding my hand out.

Linda took it, but her expression was neutral, and her shake was firm. But Dave was giving me a sour look. I shook his hand too, and he gave me a brief nod.

"Henry and Carter are headed over," Dave said, then motioned to the chair. "Go ahead and sit. You almost died, you shouldn't be out of bed anyway."

"That's what I told him," Emily piped up.

I felt Jessica's fingers dig into my side where her arm still was. A signal? Nerves? Or did Emily bug her more than she let on?

"You must be famished," Linda said suddenly.

"I'm a bit hungry," I admitted, because as soon as I heard that, my stomach rumbled, reminding me I hadn't eaten much in a long, long time.

"I can hear your stomach from here," Dave said. "I packed some food in case you were ready," he said, putting his rifle down on the couch across from us and taking his pack off.

He dug in his pack and pulled out a soft sided cooler. I watched, not knowing what he was about to pull out, but my mouth was suddenly watering, and my stomach rumbled once again. A Tupperware container of what looked like a thick stew was handed to me. It was almost hot through the plastic, but he wasn't done. He pulled out a plastic bag with two thick slices of what looked like Texas Toast, a bread that was sliced close to an inch thick and toasted, covered in butter. My mouth was drooling, much like I imagined Diesel's did. I set the bread on the arm of the couch next to me by my left arm and then tried working the top of the stew off.

"One handed won't work well for you," Jess said, "want a hand?"

"I... sure," I admitted, realizing that without my left hand in use, there were a lot of things I was going to have to figure out how to do one handed until it healed.

Jessica took the stew and popped the top. "Dad, pull the table closer, would you?"

Dave pushed a small, rough coffee table that had been built out of plywood and two-by-fours closer to me until it was almost touching my knees. Jessica put the container on that, and Dave produced a spoon from his lunch bag.

"Thank you," I said simply and dropped the spoon in.

"Westley..." Linda started, "your grandpa was able to trade us several gallons of high proof ethanol yesterday, but Henry is wanting you to make some things for us while you heal up."

"I'll help where I can," I said, leaving that open for interpretation.

"He's worried that you're going to run out before paying your debt," Dave said, sitting down across from me and pulling on his wife's hand.

"My debt?" I asked, shoveling potato and venison stew in my mouth as fast as I could.

"Medical supplies, time, resources..." Dave continued.

"Dad, this isn't the time, he just woke up," Jessica cut in, her voice sharp.

"Don't start, dear," Linda said to her. "None of us would be in this position if you hadn't gone after him."

Her words pissed me off. My hands started shaking as I paused, a spoonful of food halfway to my mouth.

"He would have died if I hadn't gone after him, and none of the prisoners would have escaped." Jessica's words dripped in poison.

"And according to the pact we all signed onto, community resources must be decided by majority vote, or Henry's word, before they are used up."

"He would have died," Jessica said again.

I put the food down. I wanted it, but not if the guilt and strings were going to be overwhelming.

"What do you and Henry want me to do?" I asked Dave, my words acidic.

"What Duke was talking about. We have defenses in place, but no way to make more. We'd like you to make some stuff up for us. Help us make antibiotics to replace what we used on you. Making a sterilizing solution, among other—"

"For digging a bullet out of my shoulder and giving me a couple shots of penicillin?" I asked, my voice rising.

Linda put up her hands as if to placate me. "It's not our decision."

"So, I get no say in this?" I asked, amazed.

"Well—"

Emily was looking between all of us, very still. "I have to check on Mary."

I waited until she was jogging up the steps and then turned to face Jessica's family. "I'm not even awake for a full day and you're putting conditions on my care, talking about a debt I owe everyone here?"

Linda swallowed, but Dave stared at me. I decided the food I'd eaten wasn't enough. I didn't care what they thought; I started eating again, waiting on them to speak.

"It's not like it's much," Dave said, breaking the staring match and blinking first, "and it's stuff that's probably pretty easy for you to make."

"Sure, and you guys could do it too," I said, shoveling food in again, ignoring the heat of the stew.

"We don't know how," Linda said.

Jess let go of my side and pulled her arm back. I'd almost felt like I was getting squished, but I could see the tension in her, the veins in her neck standing out.

"Sterilizing solution... Get some bleach, add some water. Boom. Anesthetics, take some of that high-proof moonshine, mix that with bleach, and you have chloroform and a strong acid. Separate them and be done with it. Antibiotics... I've never done that, but with the right books, I can figure out how to grow a strain and make a slurry, but—"

"You aren't required to," Jessica told me, interrupting my tirade. "You're still laid up."

"And I'm going to need to get back to my family," I said simply, "soon."

Footsteps from the stairs had us all turn as Carter, Henry, and Mary came down, followed by the dogs.

"Not until you're medically discharged," Henry called.

"Where are my guns?" I asked Jessica with a hiss.

She shot me a look, then turned back to her parents who were looking at me with a puzzled look; evidently, they hadn't heard me.

"Not now," she whispered back sweetly, louder than I had been talking, and patted my knee as Henry walked in.

Everyone stood to shake his hand, but I remained seated, shoveling food in my face. I gave him a nod, already hating the man. Debt? I hadn't asked for anybody to follow me into the Crater of Diamonds. They had made it plain that they were not going to help.

"Glad to see you up and around. We could use a man like you around here," Henry said.

"Oh yeah?" I asked him, noting he had a softer tone in his voice than he'd had earlier.

His words as he'd walked in set me off though. I hadn't appreciated the implication that they weren't going to let me go until I was 'medically discharged'. Bullshit.

"We could. Losing the pharmacist to those people really hurt us. He was good at making some of the things he couldn't outright sell to us, but with his death..."

"You are wanting to do some horse trading by the sound of it," I said, trying to keep the annoyance and anger out of my voice.

"Eventually, once you repay our kindness," Henry shot back, sitting on the third couch so we were all looking at each other.

Carter looked out of place as he stood there. Jessica was grinding her teeth, I could hear it from here and wondered if others could too. Her jaw was pinched tight, and she was sitting so still that I could almost feel the tension emanating from her. Her parents were looking everywhere but at me and Henry.

"Want to sit, Carter?" I asked him, motioning to all the empty spaces.

"Actually, I need to check you out," he said, coming over to me and pulling his medical bag off his shoulder.

Dude was still big, but nowhere near the mountain that Duke was.

"Go ahead," I told him and sat back, taking Jessica's hand in my good one.

Henry made a sound, and I stared at him until Carter stood in front of me. He shone a flashlight in first one eye, then another. I grunted as he grabbed my left arm, under my shoulder, and felt around the open wound. I gritted my teeth as he poked and prodded and did deep breathing exercises as he listened to my heart rate. Finally, he checked out my head, tracing the stitches with his fingers.

"It's healing up well," he said, "and the stitches come out in a few days, as long as you don't tear them open again. Concussion is still affecting balance? Dizzy? Headaches?"

"Yes, to all," I told him, breaking eye contact with Henry, looking at him, now blocking me from my food. "My head feels like a rung bell."

"Did they tell you how bad you were hurt?" Carter asked me softly.

"Said I could have died?"

"Yeah, the shock was bad. I thought that alone

would have killed you, but once we were cleaning you up and you were going in and out of consciousness, I started working on your head. You know you cracked..." he motioned to my head.

"Figured it was something bad, the way you guys keep avoiding the issue."

"Cracked your skull. We were worried that the swelling wasn't going to go down. Without trained people and equipment, all we could do was keep you hydrated and drugged up, so you didn't thrash around and hurt yourself and pray."

"I really almost died?" I asked, scared.

"I thought you had," Jessica said, giving my hand a hard squeeze.

Carter sat down on the same couch with Henry, but at the other end. I noticed everyone was keeping a distance from the fiery older man. He had to have been in his sixties, but he seemed to exude confidence and something else I couldn't put my finger on. His voice carried. It wasn't big or deep like Duke's was, but there was a note of command in every word he spoke.

"Which is why we could really use a guy like you," Henry said.

"Well, like I said, sounds like you want to do some horse trading. I'm open to hearing your offers," I told him, hoping my repeated words would set the tone for what I was hoping would be a short conversation.

Jessica and Duke had been right though—I needed

more help, and my grandparents wouldn't have been physically capable of taking care of me. I lost two more days as soon as I'd got here. Somebody had to have been feeding me, helping me to the bathroom, or cleaning me up if... I didn't want to think about that.

"I figure you owe us a good two- or three-weeks' worth of work already. Once that's done, we can work out some kind of trade. Once you're healed, that is."

Linda seemed to wince, and Dave just stared at me, then down at his shoes.

"I used up enough supplies to indenture me to three weeks' of servitude?" I asked coldly.

"It's not just supplies; it's expertise, repayment for our people's injuries, then what we had to do with the people you set free. We couldn't just put them on the road without a token measure of supplies."

"You sent them away?" Jessica and I chorused.

"We don't have the supplies to take care of twenty or thirty people. I suspect many of them are going to return to their homes."

"To get swept up by the gangs again?" I asked, acid dripping off every word.

"Mom, Dad, did you know this?" Jessica asked before anybody else answered.

"Yes," David said, his eyes locked on her.

"You people are just as horrible as I thought you were," I said, looking right at Linda. "You're almost as monstrous as Lance's people."

I wobbled to my feet and grabbed the bag with the toast.

"Where the hell do you think you're going?" Henry asked.

Without turning, I said, "Apparently I have a cracked skull. I just woke up from a medically-induced or unnatural coma. I'm tired, and I'm frankly full to the brim of your bullshit."

I tucked the baggie in the sling and used my good arm to brace myself as I neared the hallway that led to the bathrooms and the closet room I had awoken in. I heard an argument break out behind me, lots of angry voices rising up. This was not how I wanted things to go, and the hurt look in Linda's face as I told her what I really thought of them felt like a pyrrhic victory. I felt bitter, vindictive, but I wasn't wrong in the end.

16

I IGNORED the knock at my door and pretended to sleep, right up until they knocked again, and I heard Raider bark.

"Come on in," I said to the darkness.

Now that my eyes were used to it, I could see inside my room despite the darkness. The glow from the light coming under the door was enough for me to see somebody was standing in front of it. The door cracked open, half blinding me, and a furry shape came in, making happy whining sounds.

"Come here, buddy," I told my pup who was already complying with my request.

He rubbed his head on my leg. I rolled and sat up awkwardly, running my hand through his coat, and looked to see who had brought him. I was expecting Jessica or Emily. Instead...

"Wes, listen..." Linda said, walking in the room and closing the door behind her. "I don't think you're being fair, and you've put my family in a horrible position."

"Good buddy, Raider," I said, ignoring her.

Even though my arm was still in a sling, I rolled my shoulder experimentally. No lightning bolts of pain shot out, nothing tore loose, no sudden blood flowed out. I did it some more. It hurt, but the more I worked at it, the less sore the joint itself seemed. Sure, the open gunshot screamed in pain, but having my entire arm in a sling helped. I wondered if I still needed it and unclipped it, pulling my arm out slowly.

"Wes, you shouldn't..."

"I don't know how you put up with these people who claim to be patriots, yet would indenture me for help that I never asked them to give. What's a country boy to do?" I asked my dog, being deliberately rude.

Raider made a chuffing sound and crawled up on the cot with me, taking up most of the open area.

"That isn't what we're doing here," Linda hissed, "but we've got rules we all agreed on and abide by."

She was shaking, her shadow almost jumping in exaggeration.

"Then they have the audacity to suggest I don't have a choice of whether or not I help them." Raider leaned into me, sharing his support and being a great listener. "But what I don't think they realize is that I was willing to die to do the right thing. Now I find out they've basically turned those people loose to fend for themselves."

Raider made a low sound in his chest, rubbing his head on my bad arm, lower near my elbow.

"My daughter almost died trying to find you, and save those people... you didn't—"

"And yet my girlfriend's mother yaps her gums, plays lip service to some old washed up dickwad who orders everyone around. I wonder what's in those rules or covenants of this MAG that's making everyone so jumpy?"

"Westley, dammit!" Linda's voice was loud. "We don't have a choice. You and Jessica forced us into this situation."

I finally turned to her and pulled out what I'd found in my backpack earlier from underneath my pillow. My pistol. I laid it on the cot to my right, out of way of the dog, but close, should I need it in a hurry. Linda saw that, and her eyes got big.

"You're... Everything was supposed to be... Locked up in the armory."

"My grandfather's hush puppy, and the M4 I picked up?" I asked her.

She nodded but had thankfully gone silent. I didn't point the gun at her, nor did I make a threatening move. All I did was pet my dog and let the pistol sit on the cot.

"I wondered where my pistol had gone. Seems

more than my rifles went missing as well. I had a set of night vision gear and spare batteries and charger go missing from my pack as well. Imagine my surprise to find my pistol had been carefully rolled up inside a button-up shirt I'd loaned out to somebody."

"Jessica." Linda's words were almost a whisper.

"Maybe she suspected what you guys would do. Or hell, maybe she flat out knew what you were going to do. She's obviously not happy about the situation but can't do anything about it, otherwise I would have left already." Not that I could have, but now I was feeling better, stronger after having eaten.

"You haven't been medically cleared," Linda said lamely.

I wondered what happened to the independent and strong woman I'd admired. I had done the guy thing and checked out Linda one time, getting an idea of what Jessica was going to look like in twenty years. She was strikingly beautiful, strong and athletic and yet utterly falling apart in front of me. Her face was tear streaked, her upper lip trembling.

"You don't seem to have a real doctor here," I told her shortly, "and I'm not in your damned army, militia, or whatever the dumb shit you call this is...?" I pointed toward the semi-circular room. "And if it really comes down to it, are any of you going to stop me when I decide it's time for me to leave?"

Linda was looking at the crate I was using as a

table, probably looking for a place to sit, when her head was jerked back roughly as somebody savagely yanked her ponytail. Linda shot an elbow backward, but Emily, the much smaller woman, had already moved to the side and let go of her hair. I had an idea what Linda was capable of, and as much of a badass as my girlfriend was, everyone seemed to respect and defer to Linda. What was her background and story? All this flashed through my mind as I reached for the pistol. What I planned on doing, I had no clue. Scare her into stopping? I never had a chance.

Raider blurred into motion, growling and snarling. I almost called him off, but he'd already barreled into Linda, bowling her over with his bulk. He was probably nearly as big as she was, but she was older and more experienced. Emily and she were knocked back into the hallway, and the young mother hit the wall while Linda bounced off her. Raider backed into the doorway, barking. I heard slapping feet coming from my left-over Raider's racket.

Emily was the first to her feet and stood in the doorway next to Raider. Linda got to her feet, looking at her arms and then brushed her hands over her sides. She was looking for Raider to have left marks or punctures on her. He was abnormally gentile, all things considered.

"Raider, come," I said in the loudest voice I could muster without shouting.

He quieted and then ran the few short steps to my side and sat in front of me.

"What's the matter with you?" Linda asked Emily who edged inside of my room, rubbing the back of her hair while splitting her attention between Raider and the small woman.

"I heard what you said to Henry and your husband. You've got no business trying to justify yourself to Wes here. I know you think I'm touched in the head, but I want you to know that while I appreciate you taking care of me and my daughter, I won't allow you to use and abuse Westley. I've had enough of that shit in my life."

The little woman's words were a snarl, and a small voice squealed in fright. Mary ran into the room, not seeing her mom just inside the doorway and focused on Raider, calling for her mom. Raider had a chance to whine briefly when Emily caught Mary from behind. The little girl let out a surprised scream then calmed as Emily spoke to her softly. Raider turned his attention back to Linda, but he was silent.

"I don't have a choice," Linda said, rubbing the back of her neck and head, "and if you touch me again, you're going to regret it." Her words matched the cool, calm persona she usually wore, but she wasn't frowning. Instead, a smile tugged at the corner of her lips.

"If I do, I'm not going to be giving your hair a tug next time," Emily said as she put Mary down on the cot next to me and brought herself up to her full height, back ramrod straight, "and I meant what I said. I will not allow you to—"

"What's going on?" a breathless Jessica asked, filling the doorway.

I HAD EATEN AGAIN AND HAD GONE THROUGH everything in my backpack. Linda left when Jessica showed up, and she and Dave seemed to have left the communications bunker entirely. Now it was just Jessica, Emily, Mary, me and the dogs. We were all sprawled out on the couches. Normally we wouldn't have been having the conversation in front of the little girl, but Diesel had sat next to her and she'd fallen asleep on the big dog. Raider had gotten on the other side of her, laying across her legs and feet like a living furry blanket. All of them were snoring, except Yager who was between Jessica and I on the couch.

"What is this agreement that ties your family's hands?" I asked Jessica for the third time.

"We're not supposed to talk about it—"

"Jessica," Emily interrupted, "if your family is going to hold all of us hostage until Westley works for them, we ought to know why."

Jessica let out a big sigh and then looked at the stairs before returning and looking at us.

"And I thought your family was in charge around here?" I asked, not giving her a chance to answer.

"Technically, we're supposed to be run like a town hall. Every family has a say, has a vote," her voice was soft as she looked nervously between me and Emily, "but things have changed, especially since the big blackout."

"What do you mean?" I asked her.

I was sitting sideways, and without the sling I was slowly rolling my shoulder and trying not to wince in pain. Inaction had left my entire body sore, but the more I worked my shoulder, the more mobility I seemed to be getting. I just hoped nobody noticed, beyond me not wearing the sling. It might benefit me for them to underestimate my recovery. I felt horrible about the division I'd caused here in Jessica's place, but only for her sake. I was still pissed.

"We are hardly the most setup family here in our group," Jessica said, and I involuntarily looked around before fixing my gaze on her again. "I mean, we lucked into finding this place. We moved in and made it ours right away. Apparently, there were lots of hard feelings. Some folks... They have cabins, shacks, and portable setups, along with caches in this area. Since Henry got the sublease from the timber company..."

"Was he behind the butthurt?" I asked her.

"I mean, I can understand some families here being upset that we ended up with a near free bunker.

That's why we offered to let this be the final fall back location for the group. My parents did that because they were worried if they didn't make the peace right away, we might have our own group looking to push us out of here."

Her words chilled me, but I had a question. "So, what's with the agreement, covenant or whatever?"

"So... Every family in our MAG signed an agreement. Basically, we have some community property that everyone here was required to buy into. It ensures we have the basics: medical, emergency supplies, guns, ammunition. Every family is responsible for their own food, but there are emergency stores. After we offered this place as a fall-fall-fall back location, Henry said that we should store all the group owned supplies here. It made sense, and it got people off our backs. Plus, we really do have way more room than we need. It's just that... nobody asked if they could move in with us. We only heard the complaints second hand, or whispers and snide remarks."

"So, people are jealous because your family got the market cornered in the best prepping bugout location, and they weren't paying attention?"

"Basically, or they were already setup and we lucked into something ready-made and paid for by somebody else. The upper floor is used like a community storage and meeting place, but down here is all us."

"So why did your mom...?" I sighed, I was holding a lot of anger inside of me, and it was starting to creep out in my voice. Maybe I needed to give them the benefit of the doubt some until I learned more. It wasn't like I could go anywhere fast right now. I was still too weak. "Why did she say the same thing Henry did, that I owe the community here?"

"Because when I took off after you, my mom, who, with my father is in charge of security, sent a lot of people to stop me or help me. I had no idea until I went looking for you. You'd already lit half the place on fire. I thought you would be close to the bunkhouse campers, so I was sneaking over there when one of the motorcycles blew up. Chunks of it lit everything on fire, and a big piece went through the roof of the camper."

"That's where you got these," I said, touching the now healing burns.

Yager looked at me and licked my arm as I reached over him. I gave him a good pat and rubbed his ears the way my pup liked.

"Yeah, once I saw that happen I threw caution to the wind. When I heard gunshots, I sort of panicked and pushed and tugged at everyone to get out. Nobody wanted to come at first, and some were... chained. That was when the rest of our crew showed up. We got the burning trailer emptied when Spider's guys quit fighting the fire long enough to chase after us. A couple were dinged by gunfire, but nothing major. You took the worst hit," she said, touching my forehead. "There were burns, scrapes, cuts from broken glass. I didn't get a chance to find you that night. After things blew up, I was worried that you'd..."

"No," I told her, "suicide by bomb is definitely not how I'll go out. Maybe I'll drink me a bad batch of shine or die of cirrhosis, but I don't see me ever pushing the button just to kill them."

"I'd been in touch with your grandma when I couldn't find you, and she was worried sick. She told me to follow Raider, so I got my dogs ready. He found you. Within two hours, he'd tracked you down and found you. When you passed out... I think Diesel tried to give you a bath himself. I'm sorry it took me so long."

"That's ok," I told her quietly. "I was nowhere close to where you thought. I was trying to be unpredictable."

"You sure were," Emily said, surprising us. I'd forgotten she was still there. She'd been sitting quietly, listening.

"So, because your group used a ton of medical supplies on me and others in your group saving the others, Henry feels like I owe you guys?"

"Basically," Jessica shot back, but it looked like she'd just bitten a lemon.

"Were you the one who put my pistol in my pack?"

Jessica grinned. "I did, but I hid it better when Duke and I got to the main road and we were told to get your stuff and take it back here. I wanted you to have a pistol close by; you never know when you're going to run into bad guys."

"Too right," I said, looking at the stairwell.

"My dad's furious. He's so mad I can't even tell you without cussing a blue streak that you had Raider knocked my mom down and pull a gun on her. Why?"

"He didn't pull a gun on her, he had it on the cot, at least that's what I saw after our fight," Emily interjected.

"What?" Jessica asked.

"I was upstairs with Mary when I overheard Linda talking to that Henry fella. She said she'd make sure Wes repaid the community, even if it meant keeping him right here. He could do his mixing on the lower level in the... mail room?"

"Where we lowered Wes down into. It's got lots of ventilation. It's how we get bulk supplies down here when we can't bring it in the front."

"Well, I got my daughter and headed downstairs. I was going to warn Wes before your mom got there, but my daughter had to pee. When they are that little, they wait until the last second, so I told her to go and then came here anyway. I heard your mom trying to justify what she was about to do and sort of lost it. I yanked her hair back. I was pissed. I've put up with a lot in my life, but I just had flashbacks of my husband being manipulative like that and—"

I stepped in with an explanation. "She pulled your mom's hair, and Raider tried to break it up. He body checked your mom. Don't worry though, if your mom's elbow would have connected on Emily, things may have been even uglier."

"Well, now my dad's saying y'all can't stay here, he won't have it. Mom's worried Henry is going to override my dad and take this place if he won't. Then he'd keep you here, and you'd build the bombs and chemical stuff they want. It's all so... complicated and scary."

I wasn't scared, more like infuriated, but I now understood things. Jessica's parents were completely isolated here. It sounded to me like Henry had used their good fortune of finding the abandoned communications bunker against them, and had the community supporting him. In a way, Jessica's family was being used as much as what they wanted to do to me. Play ball or be thrown out. In my case, play ball or stay here anyway. I was pretty much a prisoner in a gilded cage as much as they were.

"What about the men who were coming to join up with Spider and Lance's people?" Emily asked.

I sat forward. I'd completely forgotten about them in the craziness that life had been.

"They met up with Spider and Lance's guys. Yesterday they started pulling the burned-out campers out. Then they brought in more. It looks like an RV lot over there now. Anything that will run is being brought in, each carrying at least a few people. Somebody is always at the hand pumps, and there's no way we'll be able to get near them again. Somebody brought in a dozer and scooped out a big hole, then they pushed all the dead bodies into it. Into what? It's…"

"With all this going on, I need to be home with my grandparents," I told her. "They don't have anybody else, and I need to be able to—"

She stopped my words by leaning forward and kissing me. "I don't know what to do," she said after a few moments.

Emily snorted, amused or disgusted, I didn't know.

"I don't mind helping out, but I don't owe Henry or anybody three weeks of my life," I argued.

"I know, and I told him that. Repeatedly."

"What did he say?" I asked her, turning when little Mary let out a comical sounding snore.

"It wasn't my choice; it was a community choice." Her words were soft, and her lips trembled as she fought back tears.

"The community voted to hold me prisoner?" I asked her.

Jessica turned her head, her shoulders hitching. Was she crying?

"Sounds like a big load of bull to me," Emily said. "What about Mary and me?"

"Your debt is on him," Jessica said without turning.

"The hell it is," Emily muttered.

"I..." Jessica started to say something, but her words trailed off.

"What happens if I leave?" I asked her.

"They'll probably come after you," she told me quietly.

"You, the dogs?" I asked her.

She shook her head. "I'm here because of my parents. I didn't sign anything. I'm against this, but my parents... and what happens to my parents when I refuse to help? Are they going to hunt my family down too? Everything was fine here until we pulled those women and children out." She was looking at Emily as she said the last.

"You mean, that's when Henry started pushing to have Westley start working for you guys?" Emily asked, with Jessica giving her a slow nod.

"How do we know anybody is going to be hunted down?" I asked her. "They might just let me walk without repercussions."

Big words, and I winced. I was used to speaking more plainly; it let people underestimate me. Just went to show me how much I trusted her, despite everything.

"Right after things went sideways, a... nephew by marriage of one of the couples was caught stealing from somebody else. Something stupid, pain pills?

Anyway, Henry got the families worked up and called for a vote. The kid who was barely twenty was told to leave, and they packed his bags, looking for the bottle he'd stolen."

"That sounds reasonable actually," I said, wondering how this was a bad thing.

"Well, Henry was gone for two days after that. We wondered if something happened to him when he showed back up. He threw a bottle of pills to Carter and told him to return them. Then while out on patrol, Diesel, Yager, and I found the kid's body."

Her voice had gone quiet. "He'd been shot in the back and rolled over and knifed. I don't know what happened first, but it took him a while to die. I'm almost certain it was Henry and maybe one or two others who tracked him down to get the medication back."

"Why don't you do something? You were a cop before."

Jessica looked down. Never had I seen her look so defeated. "Because it would put my whole family in a bad position."

I nodded, understanding that completely.

"So, what are we going to do?" Emily asked, looking between me and Jessica.

"With all these people near my grandparents, I need to be there," I told them.

"Wes, how are the four of us and three dogs going to escape? I just don't see it working."

"You're coming too?" I asked her, grinning despite the grim situation.

"I know you'd go to hell and back to take care of your grandparents. I'm not going to let them use me to get to you. Hell, they'll probably try to use my parents to try to get me to get to you, so I might as well leave now. You have room for a former MP and some mutts?"

I grinned, then Emily got up from her couch and plopped down beside Jessica and gave her a big hug. "We can do this."

"When?" I asked aloud.

"I don't know. Henry is coming back tonight or tomorrow. Apparently, you mentioned all the stuff you can do with bleach to my mom, and he's excited for you to get started."

"Like I said, I don't mind helping," I told her. "Maybe I should get started on some stuff. I can help with the anesthetics if chloroform is ok? I've got no way of making narcotic anything..."

"And we wait for our opportunity?" Emily asked.

"I guess?" Jessica said softly, wiping her face before turning to me. "What do you need exactly?" she asked.

"My chemistry books from my grandparents' place, some glass containers to mix in and store stuff, something glass to stir with, light, and different chemicals."

"What kind of chemicals do you need?" Jessica asked me.

"Depends on what they want me to make. How about... bleach, ammonia, vinegar, turpentine, acetone, hydrogen peroxide, and ethanol... er... high-grade moonshine..."

Would anybody be able to suss out what I was thinking? I was asking for way more than I actually needed to make a simple chloroform. There was so much I needed to effectively do this, but I was developing an idea on how to get out of here. I just had to get my hands on the ingredients and get everyone outside. If I only had me to worry about, I'd have taken off right now and taken my chances. If I did that though, it would put Emily, Mary, Jessica and her parents in a danger I wasn't sure they deserved to face because of me.

Things were confusing, but I was starting to form a plan.

17

I HATED NOT BEING at one hundred percent. My shoulder ached, but I was able to work. I'd made some chloroform in small batches until my chemistry books were brought over from my grandparents. They didn't lay out what to use and how much like a cookbook would, but I could look at things, refresh my memory, and suss out a way of experimenting without blowing myself up or burning the joint down. I didn't want to do that. Not yet.

"Oh man, how can you stand the smell?" Emily said, coming in the 'mail room', the place with the metal chute they'd used to lower me down here.

"I've got a gas mask on," I reminded her, pointing to my face.

"Uggg, ok. I'll go find one," she said and turned to leave.

I made sure the fan was blowing fumes up and out, and that the reaction was finished before following her and closing the door behind me. The door clicking startled her, and she turned as I pulled my mask off.

"Boo," I said.

She smiled at me, like she was suddenly shy.

"I was wondering if you'd like to take a walk with me. Outside?"

"Where's Mary?" I asked her.

"Working with Jessica and the dogs," she said, which also answered my next question.

"Dave and Linda?"

"We've got the joint to ourselves." She playfully punched my good arm.

"Oh, what trouble we could get into." I kept my face and my words deadpan.

Her eyes got big and then she busted up laughing. "You're kidding me again," she said.

"Only a little bit. Sorry."

"No, no. I spent my entire adult life around one guy, most of it in isolation. I'm just... and you know..."

"I know," I told her. "I don't mean to be flirtatious," I admitted, punching her on the arm lightly. "Besides, I'm pretty sure my girlfriend could beat both our asses at the same time."

"She's a badass. I think she's really worried about her parents. What's their deal? Why don't they fight back against this Henry guy?"

"I'd almost forgotten, but Dave had some kind of heart surgery, then a stent put in the month before the big blackout."

"Oh... so he's really not that healthy?" she asked.

"No, and he's got his own stockpile of medicine, but it won't last forever. If they don't get into the medication the pharmacist had squirreled away in the community pile of stuff..."

"He'll die without it, won't he?"

"I think so," I told her as we entered the large semi-circular room.

"No wonder they're all scared stiff. In danger of losing their house, in danger of losing Dave. I was really pissed at Linda."

"I was too, until my head cleared, and I talked to Jessica some. Then the puzzle pieces started to fit together. They're as much prisoners here as I am. I really wish you'd take little Mary and head for my grandparents' place."

We started up the stairs, and I was using my left arm to hold the railing. Food, light physical therapy, and rest had done wonders to get me back on my feet. I was still prone to dizzy spells, but Carter told me that, in time, those would probably go away. The fact that I'd even woken up was a miracle in of itself. Since I'd finally woken up and confronted Henry, a few days had passed. I'd been working nonstop, giving the products of my labor over as soon as I was done. I'd even hand copied instructions I was planning on using to isolate some penicillin I was growing.

The process was simpler than I had imagined. I'd used hydrochloric acid, a byproduct from making chloroform with bleach and alcohol, to lower the PH of water to about a five or five point five. What I'd done then was allow bread to get moldy in a sterilized container until it was full. Then I would pour the water over it to make sort of a slurry. I'd add in enough to completely cover things. After a week, the penicillin would float to the top. Or, at least, whatever mold grew. It was highly inaccurate but isolating what killed bacteria in a homemade agar mix would allow us to further separate and refine the process and strains until we came up with a good strain to keep and keep feeding.

I honestly didn't mind helping spread that knowledge around. I'd done enough biochem in high school and college that this was right up my alley now that I had changed my entire way of thinking about chemistry. With a pang, I wondered what life would be like for me if the solar storms had never happened, and I'd gone to work in a classroom setting.

"I can't leave you here. I owe it to you to see you clear," she said, taking my hand for a moment, giving it a squeeze and then letting it go.

"But you could be putting your daughter in danger too," I said, bringing up the old argument again.

"If I thought she was in danger, I'd leave. Somehow, I don't think anybody here would be capable of hurting her, physically or emotionally."

I'd met some of the families here in the last day and a half. It was at a communal dinner and campfire, but the talk was strained, and I'd gotten lots of strange looks. Some folks who were more open were those I'd met before. Carter, some of the folks who went into the fire to free the women and children. One thing they had in common though, was none of them had kids who were younger than their teenage years. Mary was quite literally the youngest and smallest of all. Plus, she was as cute as a button and hugged everyone she met.

"I hope you're right, but I wish you'd get on down the road," I told her quietly.

"Worried about paying off my debt?" she asked, bumping me with her hip.

I grimaced after bumping the wall, but the pain was nothing like it had been. I turned, and she had taken three fast hops to the landing ahead of me.

"Listen, I—"

"Got you," she said, laughing, and took off running.

I sighed, but I was smiling. She was playful, and now that everyone knew she had a thing for me, everyone was joking with Emily and I about it, including her. Most of the time Jessica was pleasant, but sometimes I got the impression she wasn't so happy; as the bruises on my side where her fingers had dug in the other day showed.

The stairs went up two landings before a third stretch of stairs brought us to the main floor of the small bunker. I figured the facility was maybe forty feet tall overall, with both floors and some mechanical space between them. I made it to the top floor, breathing a little heavy, and looked around. The team who'd brought me here were standing near a roll-up door that had bars welded across the back, holding it locked shut. Access was through a plain looking steel door. There weren't as many lights on this level, casting much of it into shadows. Large fuel and water tanks were left behind, and an area where something mechanical had leaked oil set, the metal brackets inlaid into the cement.

Conduit and wires were all across the wall and ceiling, but they told me that when the facility was abandoned, everything was disconnected and scrapped out. Emily ran ahead and was kneeling at Mary's side, whispering to her. Mary was holding Jessica's hand as she'd been working with the dogs, but away from the group of men and women who were eyeballing my approach.

"Done for the day?" Henry called.

I waited and walked the two dozen steps until I answered. Three walls were made of cement block, the one facing the outside was a mixture of steel and block.

"Yeah, I have to wait for things to separate out, but you should have enough chloroform to perform several surgeries. Dosing with it and administering it... well, I hope your docs know what they're doing. I can't really make you heavier stuff unless you get me something with a narcotic base or you have some kind of poppies planted somewhere."

"You know how to make that kind of stuff?" Jessica asked suddenly.

"No, but in theory, yes."

"Good, I've got a list of things we're going to be needing. We'll talk more about it tomorrow," Henry told me.

I noticed somebody I hadn't seen in a while. "Hey Jimmy, how you doing?" I asked him, walking forward and holding my hand out.

"Great, hoping to do some horse trading with you and your grandpa soon," he said, a smile on his face, his hand outstretched.

I took it and shook, seeing Carter with the group along with Linda, Dave, Henry, Duke, and some of the crew I'd met already.

"How's my grandma doing?" I asked Jimmy, hoping for news, because if I didn't get some soon, I'd insist on using somebody's radio.

"I dunno," he said. "I dropped her off, what... few days, a week ago?"

My body went cold, my arms breaking out into goose bumps.

"Who's staying near my grandparents while I'm here?" I asked.

"I don't—" Jimmy started but Henry interrupted.

"We've got things under control, don't worry about it," Henry said, both hands up.

I could feel the weight of the pistol in the small of my back. I'd gotten my clothing back and laundered, so I was in my jeans and shirt, and had my flannel unbuttoned and hanging loose, covering it. Despite the layers, I felt a chill again and fought off a shudder.

"Who's watching over my grandparents?" I asked the group at large.

Jessica looked between Henry and me, and took a step to me, putting her arm on my shoulder. She was about to talk but was beat to the punch.

"Wait, you pulled Jimmy and his guys back? I thought you were going to have Marcus and Bird watch them after Jimmy came back?" Duke asked, his voice a low rumble.

"Marcus and Bird have been in the communications shack," Linda said suddenly. "They've been there nonstop while the big group has been moving through the area."

"I'll ask one more time," I snarled, my voice quiet. "Who is with my family while I'm here working on your shit?"

"They are in no danger, so I pulled our men in close in case we come in under attack," Henry said shortly, his face turning crimson.

"I guess I'll have to see about that." I tried to keep my cool, but the end came out a snarl.

"You aren't going anywhere," Henry said.

I broke away from everyone. Jessica tried to hold onto my shoulder, but I shrugged her off. Emily and Mary stayed where they were for a few heartbeats then followed me. Raider bumped my side, letting me know he was there and ready to give me his support. The gun felt heavier and heavier.

"Watch me, asshole," I said without turning, pushing through the crowd.

Raider stopped walking with me, probably to wait for Emily and Mary to come. He'd catch up soon; he was never more than sight distance away from me unless I told him to stay away.

"Stop!" Henry thundered, his voice seemingly amplified.

I turned around and saw that Henry had pulled a pistol from his belt and leveled it at me. The group was deathly silent, and a corridor of bodies was on either side of our line of fire. I was caught flat footed almost a dozen feet or more from the main door with Emily, Mary, and Jessica way too close. I looked at them and saw them all looking back and forth, fear in their eyes. Jimmy, Carter, and Duke were looking back and forth in confusion. Raider? He had trotted slowly nearer to Mary, probably to make sure she didn't walk in the middle of what was going to turn into a very ugly situation. Probably close to six feet away from Henry. An idea formed.

"Henry, I don't give two shits what you think. You're not making an indentured servant of me, and I don't care if the entire community voted to keep me here. You all can go to hell! I was promised my grandparents would be looked after while I was away!"

"Vote?" Duke asked, looking at Carter.

"What vote?" Jimmy asked me, turning.

"The one where I owe you guys two- or three-weeks' worth of my life to repay you for dragging my ass out of the state park. And he's tacking on whatever you're helping Emily and Mary with onto my butcher's bill." I worked my hand to the small of my back, my hand on the grip of my pistol.

"There was no community vote," Jimmy said. "I've been back since the day after you woke up, unless it happened while I was gone. I hadn't heard about it."

"There was no vote," Duke said, turning to Henry. "What the hell you talking about, boss?"

"We wasted valuable time and resources on Wes and his harem!" he snarled, motioning to Jessica and Emily with the pistol, making everyone tense. "He owes the community reparations and repayment!"

"I don't owe you shit," I said softly. "I would have

helped you, had you asked, but you don't force a country boy none, son. You should know better than that."

I pulled the pistol loose, but kept it behind my back, near my right leg. I tensed, waiting for Henry to focus on me, only me. There was a chance of ending this without bloodshed, or at least, gunfire. Raider was looking at me intently, his entire body tense, then he looked at Henry. He hunched down, almost like he was going to sit, with his entire back end wound up like a spring. Dave pulled his own pistol, but was holding it straight down, his head on a swivel looking between us two, the color leaving his face, and a vein throbbing in his neck.

"I am working to keep our entire area safe. Part of that is keeping assets healthy and in place, where we need them!" Henry was turning so red, I thought his head might explode.

"Which means holding me captive, not holding up your end of the agreement by somebody staying with my family while I'm gone, and basically kidnapping me so I can work for you. I'm done, Henry." I held the gun loosely at my side now, though his eyes were on mine.

"You told us he volunteered," Duke said, his voice a touch higher as the tension crept into his deep baritone.

"He owes us so much, he has no choice!" Henry

raised his gun in my direction. "What do you have to say about that?" he screamed, the gun bore looking big as it lined up with my eye.

"Támadás," I screamed.

Henry's arm wavered as he tried to process what I'd said, but Raider had broken into motion the moment the command Jessica had taught me came from my lips. Raider was a golden-brown streak, and his jaws latched around Henry's upper arm. The older man went down hard, screaming, two shots ringing out.

"Shoot it, Dave!" Henry shouted, his voice shrill as he was getting shaken, the gun finally free of his grip.

I had my pistol trained on Henry now, and I was advancing slowly, half a step at a time. Jimmy, Carter, Duke and Linda jumped back. Jessica was snarling commands at her dogs, who looked like they were being rooted in place by invisible chains. I had no shot on Henry and called the halt command to Raider more than once, but the screams, snarls, and cries may have drowned me out as the sound echoed around the block chamber. I waited for my dog to get loose, for my shot to materialize.

"Shoot it!" I heard Henry scream again.

Who was he talking to? I looked to my right and saw Dave start to raise his pistol, and it wasn't pointed my way, but Henry's. Except, it wasn't. It was pointed in front of Henry. He was moving slowly, deliberately.

"Not my dog!" I screamed as my gun and Dave's went off at the same time as Jessica leapt.

My screams of horror, loss, and agony hit as the realization of what happened kicked in and I fell to my knees, my pistol dropping to the ground.

"No, no, no, no, noooooooooooooooooooooooo!"

I didn't know who screamed that? Jessica? Emily, Mary, Linda, me or...

The world went black around the edges, and the earth pulled me down, my body unable to fight gravity. I looked sideways across the ground, pools of sticky redness growing, threatening to paint my skin. I screamed until the darkness overtook me.

-THE END -

To be notified of new releases, please sign up for my mailing list at: http://eepurl.com/bghQbi

ABOUT THE AUTHOR

Boyd Craven III was born and raised in Michigan, an avid outdoorsman who's always loved to read and write from a young age. When he isn't working outside on the farm, or chasing a household of kids, he's sitting in his Lazy Boy, typing away.

You can find the rest of Boyd's books on Amazon & Select Book Stores.

boydcraven.com
boyd3@live.com

Printed in Great Britain
by Amazon

17877545R00161